EAGER HOUSEWIFE

EVIE ROSE

Copyright © 2024 by Evie Rose

All rights reserved.

No part of this book may be reproduced in any form or by any electronic or mechanical means, including information storage and retrieval systems, without written permission from the author, except for the use of brief quotations in a book review.

This story is a work of fiction. Names, characters, places, and incidents are the product of the author's imagination or are used fictitiously. Any resemblance to actual events, locales, or persons, living or dead, is coincidental.

Cover: © 2024 by Evie Rose. Images under licence from Deposit Photos and Shutterstock.

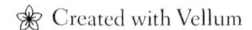

❦ Created with Vellum

1

BLYTHE

"I'm a bit worried," Ainsley confesses, pausing in rolling clothes into her suitcase to glance up at me, sitting on her bed in her father's house.

"It's natural to be nervous before a big trip," I say, and my mind flits through all the reasons we both have to be anxious. "You're travelling around the world, solo!"

"It's not that. It's my dad. I think he'll be lonely."

Ask me to go and see him, I beg her internally. *I'll listen to everything he wants to talk about. I'll do anything. I'd be perfect for the job.*

I don't say that aloud, because Ainsley thinks I like her dad in a normal way. She doesn't know about my crush, and she'd be horrified if she did. As would he, because I'm so much younger than him.

"I'm sure he'll be okay." And I believe that. Unfortunately. "He is a mafia boss, after all."

He runs the Blackstone mafia, as generations of Blackstone men have before him.

"Mm." Ainsley fiddles with a pair of pink socks. "I feel bad for leaving him behind. And you."

"I'll be fine as well." I put on a careful smile, because this I'm less convinced by. Not only is my best friend going travelling without me, my house share has fallen through, and far worse, I won't have an excuse to see the man I love more than anyone in the world: my best friend's dad. "You, on the other hand, will miss your flight unless you get stuff in your suitcase, stat."

Ainsley snorts. "Yes, Mum."

"Yeah. Well." I fold my arms and give her a mock severe look. It's a running joke between us that I try to mother her, even though we're the same age. I guess it comes with the territory of doing a degree in childhood studies and being an orphan. I'm desperate to love someone who loves me in return. A baby would be ideal, but my friend is a decent second. Especially since she's been such a good friend to me, inviting me for holidays at her house so I don't have to spend them alone, and always being up for a chat.

We have been inseparable since we met in the library while studying in the first semester of both our third years. She is super smart and got top marks in her biology degree. Whereas I did well with the practical stuff, but struggled with the written work.

Ainsley fiddles with the sleeve of a hoody. "What if Dad doesn't eat properly while I'm away?"

I shake my head. That man knows how to keep in shape, no question. And he's a billionaire. He has a chef to cook for him and his men to remind him about meals. He's forty years old and in the prime of his life. Ainsley's concern is purely fictional and a displacement from worrying about her own trip.

"You continue packing," I suggest. "I'm going to get your dad so he can tell you he's capable of remembering food is necessary for continued existence."

It's the morning, so Mr Blackstone is in his home office. The door is closed, but because he's the best of dads and never minds dropping everything for his daughter, I know that's not an issue. I tap on his door before poking my head in. Mr Blackstone has his phone to his ear and a glass of water in his hand.

For a second I'm struck dumb by his beauty. His auburn hair—much darker than his daughter's red hair—is shot through with a hint of silver at the temples that adds to his distinguished look and his stormy blue eyes are surrounded by laughter lines.

You wouldn't think to look at his face that he was feared among the London mafias. But it's not his imposing height at six-foot-four, or impressive physique that scares people. It's the fact that when Ainsley was five someone tried to kidnap her. She doesn't remember it much, but she showed me a photo of an old newspaper cutting of the aftermath. Mr Blackstone killed every member of the gang who tried to take his daughter, and left them unrecognisable except by their DNA.

Guess it is true what they say about a redhead's temper.

There are faint lines of scars across his knuckles from the hours he spent exacting that bloody revenge. Sometimes, when Ainsley is talking, Mr Blackstone will rub the faded marks unconsciously.

He looks up and his expression goes from a scowl to something that, if I didn't know better, I'd interpret as joy. Then that's wiped away and his eyebrows pinch.

"I'll call back," he says smoothly. He hurriedly places both phone and water glass onto his desk. "Blythe."

I love the way he pronounces my name, his Scottish-accented voice like warm alcohol-laced chocolate.

"Ainsley is upset." I try to focus. "Will you—"

Mr Blackstone doesn't need to be asked, he's immediately on his feet. But there's a crash and splosh as in his haste, he's knocked the glass of water from his desk.

"Shite," he swears under his breath and halts, having already taken several steps towards the door.

"Don't worry, I'll clear it up," I offer quickly as he hesitates, about to go back. "So you can see Ainsley."

"Sure?" he checks.

"Nae bother," I assure him, and amusement sparks in his eyes from me using the Scottish phrase I picked up from him and Ainsley.

"Tissues—" He gestures vaguely to his desk.

"I've got it."

Mr Blackwood flashes me a grateful smile that basically sets my knickers on fire—good thing there's water around—and is out of the door and striding down the corridor to talk to his daughter before I can so much as swoon from him being so scorching hot.

I inhale a deep, shaky breath as though the smoke from my burning knickers is making me oxygen deprived. His office smells like him, of a woodsy scent, with pine and charcoal, mixed with fresh mountain air. For the first time, I approach his desk and go around it. My heart drums with how intimate it feels to be in his private space.

The water has splashed over the carpet and his enormous black leather chair, but the glass is undamaged. I bend to pick it up, and pause as I see his computer. The screen is on, a document showing. At the bottom the cursor blinks, as though he's just stopped typing.

Position available: marriage of convenience

. . .

Seeking wife for a London mafia boss to accompany her husband to formal events, homemaking (cooking and cleaning optional, fully staffed household), make a family, etc.

Children compulsory, no contraception.

Luxury accommodation, million-a-year expenses, and lifelong security.

Must laugh at husband's jokes, be around 5'4", brunette, blue eyes. Would prefer if the applicant could get along with my young-adult daughter.

No emotional attachment.

A fake marriage. Don't expect love.

Free use. No knickers to be worn.

My eyes bulge out of my head as I read. Then read it again, and again.

The kingpin of Blackstone is advertising for a *wife*.

He's been a single father for the time I've known him, and Ainsley says she can't really remember her mother. It's always been her and her dad, and she's never mentioned any women in his life. Not girlfriends or even casual companions. And now he wants a marriage of convenience.

I could do that. The realisation lights a fuse in me.

I want it so badly my chest feels like it might explode. I keep flitting around between all the details, every one more exciting than the last.

Children. Oh my god I'd love Mr Blackstone's babies so much.

Free use. I've heard that on social media. It means he'd be at liberty to use me however he wanted, whenever he wanted. The idea should horrify me. He's twice my age, and my best friend's dad. But it doesn't. Not even slightly. Heat blooms between my legs, revealing how not just *not* disgusted I am. I'm turned on.

The thought that I could be in this house going about my life, and Mr Blackstone would just come up behind me, push my skirt up, unzip himself and bend me over the nearest surface without so much as a "please"?

The idea shimmers over my skin.

Other things are attractive too, of course. I need a place to live. I love homemaking and I'd be proud to be on Mr Blackstone's arm at any event he chose.

And the physical description. That's... Me. Exactly. I'm five-four. I always keep my hair tied back, but it is brown. I'm not pretty though, certainly no match for Mr Blackstone with his rugged good looks and sharp suits. My nose is snub, and my face is kinda oval and boring. But my eyes are pale blue, and I get along with Ainsley.

I am the perfect applicant.

Except for the obvious and prohibitive issue: Ainsley is my bestie and Mr Blackstone is almost twice my age.

At the airport departure gate, Mr Blackstone and I stand side-by-side and watch Ainsley all the way until she's out of sight. Through security. Off on her adventure to Europe.

Any second, Mr Blackstone is going to leave. I'll be alone, homeless, without my best friend, and the man I love more than anything in the world will be married—*conveniently*—to another girl, who looks like me.

So I screw up all my courage.

"I saw your advertisement," I croak.

He turns his head oh so slowly and stares down at me. "What?"

"The one for a wife." My heart flutters, a caught wild bird.

The blood drains from his face. "You weren't supposed to see that."

No. Obviously. And neither should I be doing this. I swallow hard.

"I want to apply."

2

DUNCAN

I gaze into the face of my daughter's best friend in mute horror and rising desire.

My cock is thickening, despite the impossibility of this. Blythe wants to be my convenient free use *housewife*?

"You should forget about it." I curse myself that I typed out my longing for companionship and family when Blythe was so fresh in my mind. I listed what I wanted—someone exactly like her—with the awareness that I couldn't fall in love with my potential wife because my heart belongs to Blythe.

The result? A sordid mix that Blythe should never've seen.

"I'm not going to," she insists in that sweet voice that floors me every time and makes me feel like a perverted old man.

I've never had any hint of attraction to any of Ainsley's friends before Blythe. Even now, I urge myself to look at her and see what I did when she first appeared on my doorstep. A young, pretty girl who was just my daughter's new best friend.

Last year, when Ainsley told me about the study partner she'd met and asked if Blythe could come for Christmas, because she would otherwise have spent it alone, I said yes. Of course I did. It didn't occur to me that it would cause me physical pain to keep myself decent.

Then Ainsley was delayed, Blythe arrived on the doorstep, and I was cut off at the knees by emotions as known to me as the surface of Mars, and just as survivable. Forty years on this planet and I'd felt nothing like the two of us having dinner that night. She made me laugh. She was beautiful and funny, and I kept having to tell myself that it wasn't a date.

Because I swear she liked me too. And she's come back with Ainsley for every university holiday since. Sometimes, when Ainsley isn't looking, I catch Blythe peeking at me from under her long lashes, and I indulge in two seconds of crazy that she is as compelled by me as I am by her.

And when they graduated, and Blythe had no one with her to tell her they were proud of her or cheer when she was on stage collecting her degree, I filled the gap, telling myself it was just fatherly. I said that as I bought her the expensive formal photos and clapped extra hard for her, and nodded when Ainsley asked if Blythe could come home with us and help her pack for her round-the-world tour.

"I can meet everything on your list of requirements," Blythe adds eagerly, jerking me back to the present where this twenty-one-year-old girl has read my dirtiest fantasies.

Of course she can fulfil the specification. It was written with her in my mind.

"No."

I turn and walk away.

"Mr Blackstone." She's having to trot to keep up with

my longer strides and instinctively I shorten them. Internally, I groan. "I know I'm young, but—"

"The answer is no, and that's final," I snap, and immediately regret it when I see her kicked-puppy expression from the corner of my eye.

"Okay," she says in a small voice.

I stop and rub a hand over my forehead. "What's happening next for you, Blythe?"

"I'll be fine." At my side, she wrings her hands.

Oh fuck. Nothing is more of a red flag to me than the word fine. She might as well have said "miserable" or "inadequate". Fine is shit. No one I love—and I love Blythe more than my tattered soul—will ever be just *fine*. And she sounds so unhappy.

"Come with me." I keep walking out of the airport towards the car park, and she trots behind. I'm being an arsehole, but I can't look at her. I can't stop, or I'll cave.

"It's fine—"

That word again. My hand has darted out and caught her wrist before I can stop it and I drag her out to where the SUV is parked.

"Get in." Being in an enclosed space with this girl I want in every way is a terrible idea. Really, really bad. But I cannae leave her at the airport.

She obeys and her obedience eases the tightness in my chest. A bit. "Where are you going to work? You said you had a plan?"

"I don't know." She's curled in on herself in the passenger seat beside me as I drive us out and into the London traffic.

I sigh. "When you rejected my offer to pay for you to go travelling with Ainsley you said you had a job."

I should have insisted they travel together. Then Blythe

would be safely on a plane right now, with no worries, and not next to me, like temptation incarnate.

"I didn't. I said I would *prefer* to have a job. I put a deposit on a house share, but they've all ghosted me."

"They've *what?*" I accelerate as we join the motorway, but I can barely see the road for the rage clouding down over me.

"They kicked me out of the group chat, and when I went to the house we were renting together, there were students living there."

"Fuck!" My knuckles are white where I'm gripping the steering wheel. But noticing that only makes me remember what I've done for people I love. I'm going to quietly punish whoever fleeced Blythe. Maybe a few punches as well, for good measure. My scars could do with a refresh.

"I'm sorry," she whispers meekly.

"Not you, not you. Them," I hasten to reassure her. "But I'll sort you out. You can stay at a hotel until you get yourself settled." The words stick in my throat like a sharp chicken bone. I want her with *me*.

"You don't have to—"

"I do."

"Thank you." Her voice is so soft and high, and the tremble in it causes my heart to resonate painfully.

There's a long, awkward silence during which I think about things I could say.

I didn't mean to describe you in that advert, it just happened because I'm obsessed with you. I'll buy you a home in London. Don't house share again, and don't live outside my London territory. I'll find you a job. If it weren't for my daughter, I'd take you up in a split-second on accepting my marriage-of-convenience proposal. You'd have your knickers ripped off and my cock in you before you could blink.

"I'm too old for you." I didn't realise I was going to say that, but it's true. "You should be with someone your own age." The words grate over my tongue.

"I don't like boys my age."

"You don't want... Marriage." I refuse to glance across at her and settle for that euphemism, when we both know I mean, "to be the sex toy of a man twice your age". She'd be my secretly-cherished wife though. Not convenient, but adored.

"I do." She sounds so earnest, it breaks my heart. "I'm no good at studying or most things, but..."

Jealousy grips me at the thought of her unspoken words. Not excellent at studying, but great at sex. Don't get me wrong, I'm certain she's amazing in bed, but there's so much more to her.

This time I can't hold back. I flick my gaze to the side and she's biting her lip, staring ahead at the windscreen.

"I've always wanted a home and children of my own." Her tone is wistful. "It would be really fun to have a big, loving family. So different to..." There's longing in the tilt of her head.

She doesn't need to add that. I remember. During that evening at Christmas, she told me about her childhood in the care system, flipped between foster homes until she aged-out at eighteen and was on her own.

"Really?" I ask. "You truly want to have a family so soon? No adventures first?"

"Babies are all the excitement I need," she says with a firmness that belies her twenty-one years.

A spark of potential flares. If she wants a family, and I want her, would this be so wrong? The age gap between us is filthy, yes. But if I could genuinely provide Blythe with the life she'd like...

The job advert was written on a whim. I didn't really intend to post it. But the more I imagine the scene, the more I want more kids. Watching my daughter pack up to spread her wings and become an adult made me realise I missed the vibrancy of having children in my house. I miss the noise and mess and chaos. I used to curse Ainsley, especially when she threw tantrums or asked where her mother was. Because I couldn't tell her that her mother dumped a wee fiery-haired three-year-old lassie on my doorstep and hasn't been seen since.

Ainsley going to university three years ago left an empty place in my heart. Then Blythe cracked it entirely open, and it's a chasm. Filling that aching gap with Blythe and our children is too perfect to be believable.

"I did childhood studies at university because I want to be with kids," Blythe adds. "This isn't a whim."

"What if I set you up so you could have your own house and childcare centre." I can afford it. I manoeuvre us through the London traffic, my thoughts racing. "One that you owned, and ran exactly as you liked."

There's a pause.

"Why would you do that?"

"To help you. Or..." I cannae believe I'm going to offer this. But you're a long time deid, as my Scottish grandfather used to say. "You can have the marriage of convenience. Like I set out in the advert you read."

I've lost my goddamn mind. I'll go to hell for this. I'll be rightly judged a class-A arsehole. I'll risk losing my daughter and that's a pain in my heart... But what I could gain? *Blythe*.

"I'll have marriage," she replies promptly, as though there's no question which is better.

"There'll be a prenup." It would have terms more

generous than any standard divorce settlement, but she's not to know that.

"I don't care. I don't want your money."

Her sweet voice ruins me, and as I pull up at the Blackstone house, I recognise I'm not strong enough to say no.

"There's one more thing."

"Yes?"

"We'd have to both be faithful." Not an issue on my side, for certain. "I don't share. If you're my wife, you're *mine*."

3

BLYTHE

"I'm yours." The admission sends a shiver through me, as though it's a magical vow sworn in blood rather than an impulsive truth spoken in a stationary vehicle.

I'm his. I have been since we first met.

Mr Blackstone's throat bobs as he swallows, and I wonder if he's as affected by this conversation as I am. We've stopped, but he's gripping the steering wheel and looking ahead as though we're speeding down a road, out of control.

"Two days off a week," he rumbles.

"What?"

"You have to—"

"That wasn't in the advert," I cut in. I don't need holidays as though this is a nine-to-five in a grey office.

I want surprise gleeful loving hot sexy times, at any hour of any day. No, I haven't got specific ideas about what that really entails, but that's beside the point.

"I hadn't finished writing the specification before you…" He pauses and I cringe, biting my tongue to prevent myself from saying that I didn't mean to snoop. "*Saw* it."

"Right." I'm not disappointed. I'm not. It makes perfect sense.

Although, of course I'm a bit hurt he doesn't want me to be his wife *all the time*. His *free use* wife.

"You can do whatever you want at the weekend. Except see anyone in a..."

"I won't," I say quickly. Anything he's about to specify, I don't want. I only desire Mr Blackstone. "And I don't need days—"

"You'll have time off, because I will expect a lot from you during the week," he growls, jaw set as he unpeels his hands from the steering wheel and shoves the car door open.

My heart bounces. I wonder exactly what he'll expect. I hope I can satisfy him. Can we still spend time together during my weekends off? I don't dare ask. But I hope so. I really, really hope so.

He strides around the vehicle, yanks open my door, and regards me darkly.

"Okay." My throat is so tight I'm only capable of that squeak, but it's enough.

He nods tersely, offers his hand, and when I take it pulls me from my seat. He doesn't let go as we enter the house, his big hand enveloping mine.

And that's it, I guess. We're betrothed.

I'm engaged to my crush. The father of my best friend. The man who stole my heart over the course of our first evening together, and who heats me all over every time he looks at me.

This is insane.

Mr Blackstone pulls me through to the kitchen, and I obediently scramble onto the stool at the kitchen island he leaves me next to as he sets about making coffee. His phone buzzes in his pocket almost non-stop with notifications and calls. He doesn't even glance at it.

"You can answer your phone, it alright," I say after a couple of minutes.

I don't know what to do with myself.

I basically proposed marriage to my best friend's dad, and now... There's no rule book for this.

"No." He shakes his head abruptly. "That's just Blackstone work. Nothing to be concerned with compared to..."

He pulls the phone from his pocket, silences it, and tosses it onto the marble countertop where it lies motionless. A dead little brick.

"But before we go any further, we should clarify what we both expect from this marriage."

Suddenly, I'm pinned. I daren't breathe for the risk I might shatter my chance with Mr Blackstone. Does he need me to do some clever thing? Maybe be really sexy?

I don't know how to do that. I can barely flirt or get myself off with my fingers. I certainly can't be a seductress.

"I don't want you to be under illusions, Blythe." He sets a cappuccino before me and an espresso in front of himself.

He remembers what my favourite coffee is.

"About free use, you mean?" I ask, voice wobbling.

He knocks back the espresso in one gulp and I watch entranced at the bob of his dark stubbled neck. I want to kiss that roughness.

"I'd take exactly what I wanted," he says harshly, slamming the cup down and pinning me with his gaze. "Whenever I wanted it. You'd just have to be available."

The mere idea makes me weak with need.

Yes. Take me. I'll be yours anytime you like.

"I wake up horny in the middle of the night? You'll wake with my cock in your pussy," he continues. "You're doing the laundry and looking hot? I'll bend you over the washing machine. You don't say no. You don't complain. I don't *ask*. I just take."

He says these scorching words matter of factly, and without emotion, despite how filthy they are. Almost like a challenge. He's waiting for me to rebel at what he's saying. He's the hottest imaginable headteacher, laying down the rules, and asking me if I'm going to be a good girl, or be expelled. His eyes bore into me, the blue dark as ink.

"I think..." My throat is dry, and I have to break off to clear it with a cough and then swallow. "I can do that."

I congratulate myself that I didn't throw myself on the floor at his feet, begging, with my legs open.

"Can you?" he asks softly, remaining motionless.

"Yes." But my voice betrays me, shaking and higher than usual.

I'm a virgin, after all. There's no way on earth I'm telling Mr Blackstone that, because I'm pretty sure he'd freak out and call this whole idea off. But if he leads? If he's in charge, and takes what he wants from me, I will be so happy to please him. I will be his pliable doll.

I crave being his favourite, cherished, treasured toy.

"Why don't we try a test of whether you can be obedient enough?" he suggests with dangerous softness.

I nod. I will pass with top marks. I'll do anything to satisfy him.

Mr Blackstone beckons me with two fingers slowly curled and I make my way around the kitchen island. I think I expect him to—okay, I don't know what to expect. I am Bambi in this situation. Newborn, shy, gawky, spindly legs, fur. Not that last one.

He pushes off from the marble, making a gap between his body and the countertop. I take the hint, and slip into the space before he closes it with slow deliberateness, hands on either side of me, bracketing me in.

There's no hesitation as he leans in to kiss me, because he doesn't know it's my first kiss. He thinks I've been partying at university like a normal girl. How could he know how shy I am with everyone who isn't Ainsley or him? So when I tilt up my chin it's a firm, sexy kiss that deepens immediately, his lips opening mine and muffling my gasp of surprise as his tongue sweeps into my mouth. It's carnal and possessive, and he's not even touching me but my nipples tingle with need.

"Blythe," he groans, and before I know what's happening he's wrapped his arms around me. I have maybe two seconds to feel his body pressed to me—the firm muscles of his chest and abdomen, his thighs, those flexing muscles beneath his pristine white shirt, and the shockingly hot and hard length of his erection—before he's lifted me and sat me onto the edge of the smooth, cool marble.

"Lie down."

Gingerly, I ease myself back, glancing over behind me for anything in the way, but of course Mr Blackstone has already thought of that and moved the coffee cups. My elbows, then my shoulder blades touch the stone, and with my legs draped over the counter, and Mr Blackstone standing over me, I'm bared.

His gaze bores into me as I look up at him, my mouth open. I'm his meal and he's a hungry hunter, about to cut me into slivers of his choosing and devour me bit by bit. I quake.

I want him.

My best friend's dad is going to take my virginity on a kitchen countertop. I cannot wait.

But instead of releasing his erection then pushing the

solid length into me, he leans over me, bringing his head down to press a kiss first to my knee, then a bit higher. He repeats the action, each open-mouthed kiss zinging into me.

"Oh fuck, this skirt…" He drags the soft fabric up my thighs to reveal my underwear and my cheeks heat as I remember what it is.

Not because it's sexy-embarrassing. Nope. It's plain white cotton with a little pink bow. I bought it in a practical pack of three. Could I be any more boring?

Mr Blackstone is a sophisticated older man, and I am a girl in plain panties.

"I'm sorry about…" I can't finish that sentence when he straightens and frowns at me.

There's a beat of silence while he waits, unblinking.

"Sorry about what, Blythe?" he asks eventually.

"My knickers."

"That's okay. You didn't know about my rule when you dressed this morning." He snags the waistband and I'm so nonplussed all I do is lift my hips to enable him to slide my knickers down my thighs and over my calves in a whisper of soft fabric, then off altogether. He stashes them into his pocket without lifting his gaze from the flesh he's revealed.

I'm naked to the waist.

"I meant that they're so—"

"Shh." Taking both my knees in his hands, he slowly but uncompromisingly pushes my thighs open, revealing my pussy.

Ohhh… His rule about not wearing knickers as his wife. My brain catches up and my cheeks heat. No knickers.

"You're soaked," he says with evident satisfaction. Then he leans over me again and breathes in a greedy lungful of air, closing his eyes and savouring it as though I'm a sample at an expensive perfume counter. The space between us hums with energy.

I'm hot and achy under his gaze. And *confused*. I imagined free use would be all, wham, bam, in and out? Not Mr Blackstone gently prising me open and making me tingle all over without taking anything for himself. Not him completely misunderstanding my point about my knickers and removing them as though they were a cute hindrance rather than a girlish misstep.

"I thought—"

"You don't get a say in this," he interrupts me, not even looking up from where he's staring at my pussy. "Are you trying to show me you'd be a good little free use housewife, or not?"

I shut up.

After a second, his breath ghosts my inner thigh, and he murmurs, "Good girl," before licking right over my clit.

I buck and squeal with shock.

"Uh-uh." His fingers tighten on my thighs.

He licks me again in a long stroke that's so slow it's like it's for him savouring me rather than my pleasure. It's almost too much, making me jerk and mewl.

"I'm going to make you come with my mouth, and you will take it," he orders huskily.

Oh my god. Is that what's happening here?

"I—"

"You can," he insists. "Don't fight it."

So I don't.

I bite my lip to prevent myself from blurting out anything. The sensation of his hot wet tongue on my pussy is as erotic and extraordinary and unexpected as this whole day has been since I first saw his computer screen.

The contrast of the cold stone and Mr Blackstone

between my legs drives me wild. I wanted to pretend I'm cool, this is no big deal to me. But I'm writhing and moaning. It's insane. I'm a normal, everyday girl, not someone who is placed onto a high surface and devoured carnally.

Because that's what Mr Blackstone is doing, dedicatedly.

He eats me out as though he's starving, with grunts of enjoyment like I'm the best thing he's ever tasted. His hands on my thighs to keep me still as the sensations are too much for me and I writhe. Those purring sounds he makes go right into my bones. Everything tells me—apart from his lack of actual words—that he's delighted by licking me.

I'm gasping, fisting my hands and scraping my fingers on the shiny marble. I scrabble for purchase with my feet and Mr Blackstone becomes all the stricter, holding me down and doing something magic with his tongue. My back bows as the pleasure ramps up.

Then he lets one of my thighs go, and I barely have time to realise what he's going to do before he shoves a finger into my passage and I'm coming. It's like my body was waiting to have a part of him to grip onto, and that triggers me off, spinning me into ecstasy. I pulse and vibrate and although before I've used my fingers to make myself come, this is an entirely different level.

My sight is blurred, though I don't close my eyes as the pleasure buzzes through me. This orgasm is whole body shudders.

Mr Blackstone made me come with his tongue and only one solitary finger.

I manage to focus, and find my husband-to-be with his hands on either side of my hips and his stormy blue gaze on my face. His cheeks are wet, and he's smiling with an expression that's unrepentantly smug.

He just made me come.

This is free use?

"I don't understand." My eyeline falls to where he's packing a very large truncheon. It's so big, surely it's painful? Doesn't he need relief? "Aren't we going to have sex?"

He adjusts his crotch, and my breath is stolen by how much I want him.

"Not until we're married."

4

DUNCAN

The wedding takes fucking forever. The eejit clerk at Blackstone Town Hall tries to say at first he won't marry us today because of something about banns. He backs down with a gulp when faced with a curl of my lip and a peek at the gun holstered beneath my suit jacket.

I hold myself together. I'm well behaved through the whole buying a dress and getting married thing, but all I can think about is Blythe being my *free use wife*.

For the wedding, to add to the sheer temptation of her white dress, she has her hair down for the first time since I've known her. She normally has it wound together in strands—a braid? A plait? Whatever it's called. Instead, her hair falls in soft waves to her shoulders. She takes my breath away with how unconsciously beautiful she is.

I'm obsessed. I need her. Now some lizard part of my brain has decided she'll be mine, it requires every spec of self-control to keep to the plan and do this properly. To be the husband she—well. If not the husband she deserves, then at least the husband she bargained for, and no worse.

Blythe's nerves emit from her in shaky waves. She's aiming for calm and poised, I can see that. The dress she chose from the exclusive boutique I took her to is floor length and silky, without swamping her. I long to comfort her. Everything in me clamours to pull her into my arms and tell her I'll ensure she loves me. I'd burn continents to see her smile. I gave those bastards who conned her with the house share what they deserved. What I won't do though, is overstep on the deal we made.

But despite her resolve, her movements are uneven. When the clerk draws her aside—still within my sight, and he doesn't touch her since I guess he doesn't have a death wish—her nod is firm. He wants to know if she's here of her own free will, and whatever she says makes him stiffen and frown, but he accepts her choice.

During the ceremony, she doesn't look away from me. Not for a moment. I didn't appreciate that soft, innocent blue eyes could burn with desire and nerves simultaneously, or that a mere slip of a girl could reduce me to pure desire. But Blythe does both.

Every time her gaze sweeps down to my waist, then pauses, like she's too shy to go further, my cock gets harder underneath my kilt. How wrong I am to do this echoes down my spine as she says that she'll take me as her husband, her eyebrows pinched together.

"I promise to be true to you in good times and in bad, in sickness and in health." She repeats the vows.

"And free use."

The clerk's gaze snaps to me, horrified, and the whites of Blythe's eyes are vivid in the little cream-painted room, morning sun from the window highlighting the far side of her face. He insisted "obey" was antiquated before we began the ceremony, but apparently that's not what I want, and I don't need his fucking permission to have my wife vow what she promised.

There's a second of tense silence, then the clerk begins, "With respect—"

"And I promise you free use," Blythe states, her voice shaking. But her chin has come up and her cheeks are pink.

The words are a bolt of electricity between us and right into my heart. A single nod is all the outward sign I allow myself. But inside I'm a battleground of love and lust and possessive, vicious need.

She did it. This sweet girl who's the same age as my daughter, just vowed that I can take her whenever and wherever I want. That I can slam my cock into her with no warning and fill her up with my come.

Mrs Blackstone will take everything her husband gives.

A hasty wedding is supposed to cleanse and sanctify my filthy desires, but with every gentle word I'm getting more turned on. My dirty needs are emphasised as the clerk speaks words about love and faithfulness and it's definitely wrong that when I slide her ring on as pre-come leaks from my cock. I want her now. And while her hand shakes as she pushes the thick gold band onto my finger, she licks her lips. That one movement from her is sexier than full nudity and humping from any other woman in the world.

The filthy age gap between us punches me in the gut as she signs her name next to her date of birth—the same year as my daughter—on the marriage certificate.

When the ceremony is over, I kiss her delicately, while thinking of what I'm going to do to her as soon as we're alone. She tastes of cherry lip balm and innocence.

The urge to take her right here in the soft yellow light is almost overwhelming.

She's *my wife*. The simple thought turns my cock from

its always turgid state that's my response to her presence, to solid granite. I'm throbbing with need.

The only way I keep a grip on my lust is by not looking at Blythe as we walk out of the Town Hall. The drive is a blur. I lift her from the car and carry her into the house. My brain is static and images of me and her, together, as I kick the front door shut behind us.

And that's it.

We're married. It's just me and my housewife, alone in our home, and she promised *free use*.

I lose it.

I cannot wait another minute. Not one more second. I've restrained myself, and now I've got nawt left. Zero cool.

I fall to my knees, and lower Blythe to the floor, her sweet arse bumping lightly on the marble.

"What?"

There's no sane answer I can give, so I say nothing.

She clings to my shoulders as I kick out her thighs and she gasps. I didn't realise I was going to transform into a slathering beast, but she's *mine* and I have to claim her *now*.

With greedy hands I drag her white skirt up and seize her cunt like it belongs to me. Because it does. Blythe promised me complete access.

But there's fabric barring my way.

I let out a furious, frustrated growl as I clutch the waistband and yank, uncompromisingly. The thin cotton rips and I shove it into my pocket without removing my gaze from her face.

"I never, ever want to see anything between your legs again that stops me having you." I sound crazed and animalistic even to my own ears as I grip her pussy to make my point. "Do you understand?"

"Mr Blackwell," she breathes, and I feel it. I was eager

to go down on her first, get her ready with my tongue, but it's not needed. Her soft little folds are already slick with arousal. My heart crashes against my ribcage and I'm even more desperate than before. I look into her face and shove my kilt up, freeing my erection. I brace myself on my forearms over her.

"I..." She doesn't finish that thought.

The tip of my cock is at her entrance instinctively, like we're natural together. No fumbling. I'm notched into the right place and then I'm staring into her gentle blue eyes, and pushing into her.

I'm helpless and I'm the aggressor. I'm utterly in her thrall.

5

DUNCAN

"Take it," I order her as she's too tight to push through.

A wounded noise escapes her.

I drive harder, not saying what we both know: this is what she signed up for. Free use. Any time.

She said she wanted to get pregnant, and she knew the conditions. I wanted her at the first opportunity, and that's on this cold black onyx floor.

I force my way in, watching her face for any sign of reluctance as surprise fills her eyes. Shock at how big I am and how uncompromising.

"So tight," I grunt as I press in, inch by inch. She's biting her lip until it's white, holding in the squeak of pain. But she doesn't say nae. She doesn't try to stop me.

"Breathe," I tell her, my gaze never leaving her face. Then I shove deeper, right to the hilt. She gasps and we're totally joined, as close as two people can be.

Apart from the fact we're both fully clothed.

I pause, some residual part of me not completely overcome. Blythe sucks in air and stares up at me as though transfixed. We remain like that until she gives a jolting nod. Only a quarter of an inch of movement.

It's permission, and I fucking take it.

I draw back and plunge into her, harder and faster than I should. Our bodies slam together, shoving her onto the unyielding marble. I'm harder than stone inside her, throbbing and angry. I do it again, and again, the pleasure sharp and heady. She's tight and wet and velvet. Soft, so soft, and yet gripping me like no woman ever has. She's a cocktail of drugs that make me crazier with every addictive stroke of my body into hers. I take her quicker, tense desire screwing into my spine each time I thrust.

I'm feral.

Now she's my wife, and she promised free use. I have precisely what I want. And what I want is everything.

My breath is harsh in the echoey foyer. There's the brutal slap of my skin on hers as I pound her into the stone floor.

I reach for her clit, cramming my hand into the non-existent space between us. Part of me longs to apologise. An even larger part wishes I could shout that I love her, and I'm sorry, and that I'm so obsessed I can't help myself. But sex is the only communication of my adoration I permit.

As I ram uncompromisingly into her soft wetness, I find that little nub and I stroke. The effect is instant. She tightens yet more, as though attempting to strangle my orgasm out before I can give her what she needs.

Then she breaks, pulsing around my shaft, and crying out her pleasure as she tugs at the sides of my suit jacket. I'm still watching her fathomless blue eyes as my climax barrels out, seeming to originate at the sensitive tip of my cock, my balls, my pelvis, and my heart, simultaneously.

I pump my seed into her in pulses of orgasm so intense

they shake the broken shards of my soul right out of my body and into hers. I might have extracted a vow of free use from Blythe, but as my vision blurs and all I can see is the blue of her eyes, I know it's me who is her slave. I belong to my wife entirely.

On the fourth or fifth or billionth wracking spurt, I bury my face in the crook of her neck, breathing in the bergamot scent of her shampoo, to muffle my groans and prevent myself from revealing how much more than convenient this marriage is to me.

And when that's not enough, and the pleasure threatens to stop my heartbeat, I bite. I sink my teeth into her neck, and she cries out again. I suck at her tender flesh as though I could steal back the essence of myself I'm giving her.

But I can't. She has it all.

I'm still shaking when the thought that it's over occurs to me. I've had my wife for the first time. She's warm and still beneath me.

I gather up my wits, and draw back. There are so many things I want to say. Words of love and gratitude and apology. *I love you. I needed that so much, thank you. I'll make it better for you next time, but I have to have you again, and soon. You have my heart and my soul, and I'll love you until the sun caves in on itself and becomes a black hole.*

Instead, I pull out and quickly tuck my still achingly-hard cock away.

She lets out a little startled sound and wriggles beneath me. "It feels..."

I clamp my hand between her spread legs, my copious ejaculate seeping out. Presumably that wetness is what she's surprised by. She'll have never had sex without a condom.

"Get used to being a creampie." It's a joke, and not a joke.

She huffs with gentle laughter, and I wonder if that's just because of her promise to laugh at my jokes.

I kiss her neck softly as I push my sperm back into her puffy little soaking entrance, fingering her as I do. Cupping her with one hand, with the other I lace our fingers and bring them, joined, to her slit.

"Hold it in." I look right into her eyes.

"Knickers would really help with this," she mutters. "It's all sliding out."

"No knickers." I'm firm about that one. I want her bare between the thighs any time I need her. "I said hold it in, wife."

"I'm trying!" She chokes with laughter, and I grin in response.

"My come will drip down your thighs constantly," I tell her. "I won't stop until you're bred."

"You really want to get me pregnant?"

"Nope. I want to *breed* you, my wee bonnie housewife." She's so gorgeous, I want miniature versions of her to give to the world. My gift to humanity. I cannae wait for wee bairns who look just like her. Who are as kind and sweet and funny.

"Oh." She blinks up at me, eyes big.

"Regrets?" I cast my gaze down, unwilling to see the answer in her expression.

And that's when I notice the blood.

It's only a small smear of pink in the white of our combined cream over my fingers.

"Blythe," I rasp.

The evidence is damning, pouring mercury into my stomach, a heavy poisonous metal.

"You were a virgin." And I am the worst husband ever.

"Yes?" There's uncertainty in her tone.

Duelling emotions rage in my chest. Fury that she didn't tell me, that she kept this from me. Anger at myself that I didn't guess, and I wasn't gentler with her. I didn't make her first time as sweet as it should have been, and I can never change that. I would have been as patient as she deserves, and instead I was a crazed animal let off the leash.

I took my untouched wife on the floor, without being careful or slow or considerate. I'm choked with regret. I should have *known*. She was so tight, I should have realised. I could break my own bones for revenge at how I've hurt her. My little wifey, who I only want to protect and love and worship in this fucked-up way we agreed to.

My hands ball into fists and her eyes go wary as she notices.

Forcing my fingers open, I nod, as I allow myself to acknowledge the other feeling: a spark of happiness. I am such an arsehole that I'm pleased this beautiful little creature belongs entirely to me. I plucked the loveliest flower.

She's *mine*.

Not just my wife, but I'm the only man to ever plunder her perfect body. I was the first, and if I have anything to do with it, I'll be the last and only. I own her pussy.

Free use.

She promised it in her vows, and I'll make it good for her from now on, and try to rectify my blunder. I'll have her screaming with pleasure over and over as I grind myself into her pussy and spray my come right up against her womb.

"You're not angry, are you?" Her happy post-orgasm smile has faded to uncertainty.

"Nae. But that wasn't the first time you deserved. You should have told me."

She nods slowly, and catches her lip between her teeth in a sly little smile. "It wasn't so bad."

The smugness of the way she says it both relieves me and causes a wave of recollection. The floor. I was so desperate I took her virginity on marble. And I didn't ask about her experience because I didn't want to hear about her having been with other men.

"Blythe," I say severely.

"It's true," she insists, the sparkle back in her eyes.

"No more secrets between us, ye ken?" It's bad enough that we're going to lie to Ainsley for a year. We can't be deceiving each other.

"Yeah. Understood." She smirks and mimics my accent, "I ken."

I nod, adding an asterisk in my mind for that one little point I'll never let on: that I love her. That this is the furthest thing from just a deal for me.

I scoop her from the floor with an arm beneath her knees and the other holding her shoulders to my chest. She snuggles into me, even as she obediently holds her pussy to keep all that seed inside.

The conflict in my heart continues to rage as I take her upstairs to my—nae, our—ensuite bathroom. I sit her on the edge of the roll top bathtub and test the temperature of the water as it begins to flow.

Blythe watches me, one hand clamped between her legs, her dress cascading both sides.

As the tub fills, I wordlessly gesture for her to stand and turn. The silence isn't exactly comfortable, but it isn't uncomfortable either.

I release her from the dress, I'm breathless as her back is revealed, smooth and soft. She's so fucking perfect.

As though we've slipped right into being a married couple, she moves to enable me without my asking. I slip the heavy fabric from her, and seamlessly she swaps hands to keep my sperm in. Such a good girl.

I take my time in examining my new bride. Kneeling to remove her shoes, I take in her slim ankles, the way her thighs are soft, and the peachy curve of her arse.

Her stockings get rolled down and I stand behind her, admiring her in disbelief. I don't allow myself to think of the consequences for either of our relationship with my daughter. This is my wedding day, and as sordid as my arrangement with Blythe is, I'm going to enjoy it.

And when the tub is full, I lower her into the water, and turn to go. A little tug on my sleeve stops me.

"Aren't you getting in too?"

I look over my shoulder at Blythe, and yet again, I'm drowning in her blue eyes.

How can I resist her?

6

BLYTHE

Mr Blackstone hesitates, narrowing his eyes at my request. I think for a moment he's going to refuse, but then he undresses with a disconcerting speed. I want to ask him to slow down, to give me more than a quick look at his wide chest, his pectorals covered with dark hair that trails down over sculpted abs to... I gulp as he slides off his kilt.

Gesturing for me to scoot over, he makes a small tidal wave as he gets into the bath, the water spilling over the edges and onto the tiled floor.

I squeak. "Should we—"

"Ignore it."

He fits his long legs on either side of my hips and firm hands pull me against him so I'm lying on his chest, the warm water around my legs and over most of my body, and Mr Blackstone's arms and torso at my back.

I know I requested it, but it's so extraordinary being like this with him. I need to see more, but all I have now is a view of his legs. And my god, they're so hairy. They're big too. He has big feet, and I flush as I remember what big feet indicate, and oh absolutely yes. I'm sore in all the right places from discovering the truth of that.

"Relax," he rumbles, stroking his rough palms down my upper arms, then brackets one arm over my chest.

As though I was waiting for his direction, I ease back against him further. And as I do, I think he sighs and kisses the top of my head.

I melt.

This is a dream, and I don't want to wake.

We lie like this for a while before his hands begin to wander. I watch as he explores my body. His big hands—they are covered with scars and have a smattering of silky dark auburn hair too—cup my little breasts. He's so different from me. Hairy and scarred where I'm smooth, big where I'm small, and muscled where I'm slightly podgy.

The contrasts make watching him touch me, sliding his hand down my belly with casual ownership, and rolling my nipple simultaneously, all the more erotic. He's an enormous bear of a man, and I'm his doll.

He keeps up caresses that are almost dispassionate because of his silence and that I can only see his arms and legs.

The crude way he took my virginity on the floor, so out of control, was extremely hot. But I think this might be even hotter.

Maybe because of the rising desire curling in my tummy, I don't notice at first that he's responding too. And it's only when he shifts beneath me, and his erection is an iron bar pressing into my spine, that I realise he's not unaffected. Quite the opposite. He wants me.

My pride swells in equal proportion to his huge cock.

I'm doing this right. For once in my life, I'm being what

someone needs. He wanted a free use housewife, and he's turned on by me. Little me?! I can't believe it, and yet at the same time I could shout and dance and spam it on social media obnoxiously every two minutes: Mr Blackstone has a hard-on from touching *me*.

"Blythe," he murmurs and grinds himself up into my back. "I need you again."

"Yes—"

A shrill ring stops me mid-word. Mr Blackwood curses and I shriek as he wraps his arms around my waist and lifts me out of the bath as he stands. Water sluices everywhere as he effortlessly steps out and sets me on the floor, holding me while I wobble. The ringing continues, but I hardly hear that as he leans down, and I get an eyeful of his perfect, biteable, muscled posterior.

"Hey, if it isn't my favourite daughter," he says, and my heart stops.

"Dad!" Her voice is muffled and tinny.

"How are you doing?" He drops a kiss onto my shoulder, and I dare not breathe. One word and we'd be discovered. It would all be ruined. No honeymoon time, just straight to recriminations and tears.

"How am *I* doing?! Your email said you met someone, and it's serious. You have to tell me everything, Dad!"

Mr Blackwood eases back and I turn. Our gazes meet, and this secret flickers between us. Forbidden, illicit. *Ours*.

We haven't talked about what we'll say to Ainsley any further than to agree we're not telling her while she's abroad. Until then, I'm going to pretend I've miraculously got my own place in London and since Ainsley's dad is a billionaire, she'll never know just how improbable that is. And Mr Blackstone said he would let her know he'd met someone.

We're delaying the inevitable, but in the meantime, it's a risky, thrilling game that sits as solid, cold guilt in my stomach. Ainsley is so important to me.

Mr Blackwood wraps a towel around his waist. "Well, I think you'll like her."

Will she, though?

He pinches my cheek, mouths, "Don't worry," and pads out of the bathroom.

Despite the steam, I'm freezing.

I am worried.

I take my time drying off, towelling my hair dry and examining the places on my breasts and thighs that feel different but look identical. Eventually, I have no reason not to creep into the bedroom. Mr Blackstone is slowly pacing up and down by the almost-floor-to-ceiling glass that leads onto the lush garden beyond, the late afternoon shadows spindly on the plants. The window frames the perfect combination of half blue sky and half deep evergreen.

"What's her name?" Ainsley asks, just audible to me.

"You can call her Mrs. Blackstone."

"Daaaadd!" she laughs, as though the idea of her father marrying is ridiculous.

But it's not a joke, is it?

"You'll meet her when you get home," Mr Blackstone says. "In a year."

He hangs up, and look across at me.

A year.

He's said it aloud now. We both know this will blow up in our faces when Ainsley returns. Understanding passes between us. He's still damp with bathwater, and glorious. And while that truncheon of an erection softened away while he was talking to Ainsley, as he drags a proprietorial gaze over my body, it thickens before my eyes.

"Are you sore?" he asks bluntly.

"No." I'm not sure that's true, but the bath definitely helped. And the adrenaline that's buzzing along my bloodstream dispels anything that might appear tomorrow.

"Get on the bed," he says gruffly, yanking off his towel and letting it fall. "All fours."

My brain doesn't understand immediately, then his eyebrows pinch together and no, no that's the last thing I ever want. I scurry to obey, discarding my towel and almost running to climb onto the unfamiliar bed covered with crisp white sheets. I position myself on the edge where I think he'll want me.

I expect him to be right at my back, but there's a pause. Seconds tick by, and I can't even hear his footsteps.

I'm so naked, so exposed as I wait for him. My breasts hang down, heavy and I stare at the dark wooden headboard. I've never been like this. I'm seldom bare for long, just while I shower, then it's on with cotton knickers immediately.

A chill passes over the curve of my butt, and shivers deliciously up my spine. My hair is a curtain either side of my face, and instinctively, I keep my eyes forward.

We have a year.

"Good girl." His footsteps are slow and deliberate across the room and I bite my lip to keep in a moan. "Don't move."

He places his palm on the small of my back, steadying. We've only had sex once, and already the anticipation is winding me up to the point I might shake apart from the effort of not pushing into his touch.

The tip of his length notches to me and he pushes achingly slowly into my waiting, soaking pussy. The gradual pinch of pain immediately blooms into fullness. His cock is so big.

We have one year. That's my last thought before pleasure takes over as he eases back out, then in, deeper, over and over until he pounds mercilessly into me, my tits swinging from the force of his thrusts.

I'm going to be his eager little housewife for 365 days and enjoy every single one until this falls apart.

7

DUNCAN

I have been insatiable. It has been a week since we married, and the hunger is just getting worse, unlike anything I've ever felt. Knowing I can have Blythe whenever I want should make it easier, there shouldn't be any desperation. But sex with my wife is more and more addictive. It's sweeter every time we join, and understand each other better. She lifts her knee before I grab it to deepen my penetration, or threads her fingers into my hair and tilts her chin to indicate she wants a kiss. I get her to a second or third orgasm before I shoot my load into her now.

I want her day and night. I've been waking in the dark and rolling her under me to fit us together, lubricated by my come from the late evening, before she's even awake. Sometimes a part of me hopes she won't wake up, so she doesn't understand how much I need her.

She always does.

And, bonnie lass that she is, every time—alright it's every night—she reaches for me. Either finding my hand and linking our fingers, or wrapping her legs around my waist.

I couldn't ask for a more convenient wife.

I'm looking forward to her weekend off in some masochistic way. It's almost too much, having her anytime I want. I've been a kid in a sweetshop. But equally, there's a sick feeling of dread when I drive from the Blackstone headquarters to my private house on Friday.

She's waiting for me in the hall, and we both stop, uncertain. Wearing a floaty skirt that makes me want to get to my knees before her, she looks as fresh and sweet as a daisy.

"Mr Blackstone." She sounds nervous. "When does the weekend begin?"

I cannae read her expression. I should say now. If she worked a normal job, Friday night would be her own. I'm an idiot for insisting on this. What's the right response?

"Do you have plans for this evening?"

She's already shaking her head before I can finish the question.

"There's a new show on in the West End." That may not be true, but I'll find something plausible. "It would be good to be seen there."

Blythe's pale blue eyes brighten. "Oh, so you need me to accompany you."

I need her always.

"We could start my days off at midnight?" she suggests.

"Aye." That's fair.

"Or on Saturday morning—"

"Midnight." Much as I want those extra hours, I don't compromise.

Her mouth sets in a mulish line. "Okay..." She strokes her hand self-consciously over her thigh. "I'll have to change into something suitable for going out." Then she peeks up at me from beneath her lashes in a come-hither that's half-hope, half-expectation.

"Me too." Who am I to deny my willing lassie? I close the gap between us in a few strides and wrap my arms around her waist, dragging her up my body until her face is level with mine and her feet dangle in the air. I kiss her lips gently. "Let's get changed. You might need a shower."

I toy with her wee hand as we watch the show from seats in the middle of the stalls, running my thumb over her soft skin. In the interval, I keep my palm at the small of her back, treat her to champagne and chocolates, and introduce her to some of my mafia connections who thankfully are at this opening night. That at least worked out, but the Laurent kingpin notices when I'm possessive of Blythe and pull her close as we discuss our legitimate businesses. He doesn't call me on the fact that at a moderately-bloody London Mafia Syndicate get together earlier in the week I claimed Blythe was just a convenient wife, and nothing was happening between us sexually because she's my *daughter's best friend*. Not my finest moment. Though Laurent exchanges a wry look with his wife, who was also present, and she hides a knowing smile as she chats with Blythe.

I wish I hadn't told them this wasn't real. There are enough reminders already.

While we're snug in the dark of the theatre seats, my arm behind Blythe's shoulders as we watch the second half of the show, and during a late tapas dinner afterwards, I wonder how I'm going to survive a night sleeping apart from her. If she wants that? We haven't discussed whether she needs more space.

We've chatted like old friends all week when I'm not fucking her brains out, but there's a lull and perhaps she's as unsure about this temporary alteration in our relationship as I am.

Two days of not being able to connect with sex.

Will I even see her over the weekend?

"How many kids do you want?" I tell myself I'm waiting for my after-dinner coffee to cool sufficiently that I can drink it, but honestly, I'm hyperaware of the ticking of my watch as it gets closer to midnight. I haven't had her since we went upstairs to dress hours ago, but I could, until twelve. The days when I can't have become a straightjacket in my mind. A conversation about the fiction that we can keep this up forever is the perfect distraction.

She blinks. "I didn't think that choice was in my vows?"

"I'll take your wishes into account," I say, with faux gravitas, and she giggles. It's the best sound in the world. "How many?"

"Two-point-four?" she suggests, not meeting my gaze and toying with her teacup. "Isn't that the average?"

"The point four could be tricky. How about we round up to the nearest ten?"

"Ten!" Her gaze flies to mine and I cannae tell if it's delight or disbelief. "You don't want ten children."

I shrug. "I'll compromise on nine-point-five."

"Half a child is fine, but point four isn't enough?"

"Aye. Half is enough. Just a wee one. Half a pint's worth. Will be nae bother."

Blythe laughs at my poor joke and my heart expands.

"Go on. You said you wanted kids. Have you got names picked out?" She blushes and it's my turn to grin. "You have, haven't you?"

"I may have some ideas," she mutters.

"Are we going to have enough that we should name them alphabetically? There's Ainsley. Our first could be Blair and we could work our way to Zane."

She splutters. "I cannot have twenty-five children!"

"Slacker," I tease. "That's poor dedication, but I guess we can start with one, and see how we go. We might already have done that."

There's a glow of happiness from her as she bites her lip and nods and I wonder if she's remembering how I told her I was breeding her as we had sex on the bed before she got dressed.

"What about five?" she says, tentatively.

I nod and let the question of whether she's pregnant yet slide. There's plenty of time. For now. "Five is a good number. Three girls and two boys."

"We might have five boys," she points out.

"Then we keep going until we have girls too."

"You want girls? Even though..." Her gaze slips to my hand on the coffee cup and the scars that cover my knuckles from where I beat the men who tried to hurt Ainsley. They tingle under her observation.

It's only been a week with Blythe, and some conversations over dinner with my daughter over the year before that. But already I know what she's thinking.

Admittedly, I sense her thoughts more when we're having sex, as though the physical connection intensifies all the feelings of closeness I've been repressing since I met this girl who is far too young and pure for a grizzled old mafia boss like me. When I'm inside her it's like we're so in sync, a trivial thing like an age difference couldn't get between us.

"There's always risk in any life, Blythe. But nothing I do for the Blackstone mafia will ever touch our bairns. I learned my lesson on that with Ainsley."

"Those scars…" She frowns. "They must ache."

I swallow and look down at my knuckles. The memory of the anger I felt at those bastards trying to take my wee daughter echoes, as it always does. Along with that other feeling. Knowledge that I sent a message to the whole of London about what happens to people who touch what is mine.

"They don't hurt." It's not entirely the truth. They're sensitive, and uncomfortable sometimes.

Blythe reaches across the table and takes my hand in hers. Our fingers slide together, her slim digits dwarfed by my big, scarred paws.

"I'm glad," she murmurs.

"Does seeing them bother you? I could get them covered with tattoos if—"

"No." And the honesty in her eyes when I look up leaves me in no doubt.

I'm proud of what I did, and she sees that. Those scars are a reminder not only to my rivals and enemies, but to myself.

Blackstones care for their own.

I stroke her knuckles and we shift easily so her palm is up against mine, emphasising the difference in our size. She's delicate. Young and vulnerable.

"You're so little." The memory of protecting my daughter mingles with the certainty that I'd do the same for Blythe or any of the children I hope we'll have.

"You're a giant."

"Your Scottish giant." I love the feel of her palm on mine. She might be small, but as I link our fingers together again, I don't think she knows how much influence she has over me. How she's my world.

She glances away, her expression clouded by something

I said, and I could bite my tongue out for messing this up. My last evening with her as my free use wife, to touch as I like, before her weekend off.

"What will Ainsley say?" she murmurs, withdrawing her hand from mine. Suddenly we're both staring at the elephant in the room.

I think of some of the comforting lies I've been telling myself. Lines like, *Ainsley will accept it in the end*, or *she'll be happy for us*. And I know that's not the problem. It's the lies of omission that we're both saying to Ainsley whenever she calls. It's the way I said to my daughter that my new partner was beautiful but not around for a photo while I stood in the lounge and looked at Blythe curled on the sofa reading a book.

I'm lying to Ainsley, and that cuts me up, even as the illicit nature of what I'm doing with Blythe heightens my desire.

Our relationship is the ultimate contradiction. Blythe is my free use *forbidden* wife. I can have her whenever I want, if it isn't during her weekend off that is about to start, and as long as my daughter doesn't find out. If only I could compartmentalise my affection for her as neatly as these two days. I can restrain myself physically, but my heart longs more for Blythe with every minute we spend together.

"We have a year," I reply instead. "And it's nearly midnight, Cinderella. I should get you home."

8

DUNCAN

It's torturing myself, but when we walk into the house after midnight, I ask, "Did you choose a bedroom for yourself?"

She starts and I stuff my hands in my pockets to prevent myself from reaching for her as she licks her lips.

"I didn't. I can—"

"It's up to—" We both speak at the same time. It's awkward. There have been multiple adjustments this week. The change from holding back to allowing myself to have her. The sneaking around and evading Ainsley's questions. And now, this new challenge. We'd just become familiar with each other sexually, and for two days that's off-limits.

"I thought you'd prefer..." I don't finish that sentence. Even in my head, it makes me a bawbag. Do I really think she's desperate to be away from me? She *chose* this. I gave her options, and she said yes to being the free use wife of her best friend's father.

It's too good to be true, though, and I can't help but suspect she'll change her mind. Especially if Ainsley finds out. When.

"I haven't made a bed, and it's late. Would you mind if I…"

"Stayed in our bed?" The relief is a tangible object. It's a life-ring in the stormy sea of my love. "Of course. It's your room too."

"It won't be a problem…?" she checks.

Yes. I shake my head. Yes, it will be an issue not reaching for Blythe as I have all week. But it would be far worse if she wasn't with me at all.

"Nae bother," I reassure her, and she smiles.

"I'm glad. I've never slept in the same bed with someone before you. I like it. It's warm—"

"You want me for my body heat," I say wryly.

"Yep. You want me for sex, so fair's fair."

I laugh, but it's hollow. If only she knew. I'm not brave enough to tell her I want so much more than sex from her. A marriage of convenience is what she signed up for, and I'll deliver. It's not as though there's any lack of my wanting her. I don't look as she gets undressed. I cannae give myself that level of temptation.

"You alright, lass?" I ask as I switch off the light once she's safely under the covers.

"Yeah."

In the darkness, we lie together not touching. Where I would normally pull her in to hold her next to me and rest her head on my pectoral, close enough to kiss her hair and breathe in the bergamot scent, instead I leave her in peace.

I don't fall asleep. Partly because my cock is at half-mast, and I'm willing it down as I listen to Blythe shifting on the mattress.

"Alright?" I enquire again.

"Good, yeah, good." She turns over. Then there are the

soft sounds of her lips moving and little inhalations as she almost speaks.

"What is it, wee lassie?"

"Would…" She trails off.

This is ridiculous. Will either of us ever finish a sentence ever again? We're like dunderheid teenagers. She at least has an excuse, only being two years more than that age. I'm *forty*. I've been the kingpin of Blackstone for a decade, and I've fallen for this girl like rock tossed into a loch.

"Go on."

"Would you be able to spend tomorrow with me?" she says in a rush, as though she'd been holding it in. "I know you don't normally have weekends off from work, but I don't have many friends in London, or full stop to be honest, and I—"

"Yes. Of course." I turn towards her, propping my head up on my hand to look down at her. The curtains are closed, and I can only see the outline of my wife. "Yes." She needs company, I'm there. "What do you want to do?"

"I don't mind."

Sweet lass. "Stop me when I get to something you like. Shopping on Oxford Street?"

"You've already bought me more than enough clothes!"

Aye, but spoiling her is such a pleasure.

"Sightseeing in London? Trip to the beach at Brighton? Fly to Paris?"

"We don't have to go anywhere special." She says that as though *she* isn't important, and I bite my tongue.

Nothing special, huh?

"How about we visit the house in Scotland?"

"Oh!"

Warmth seeps out from my heart. Yes. I found the right thing. "Dinnae Ainsley tell you about the castle?"

"Castle? No. She mentioned Lochside."

Things have been so busy, we haven't been up to Scotland since Ainsley and Blythe have been friends. "We'll go tomorrow, if you'd like."

"I would," she whispers.

A few presses on my phone, and I arrange the helicopter to take us to Lochside and for the house to be readied for its new mistress. My wife.

"Done." I click my phone off and lie back down.

"Thank you." Blythe's hand reaches out under the covers and finds my bicep.

"You're welcome."

"Do you mind...?" She wriggles nearer, and I adjust my arm until she's snuggled into me.

Just for warmth, I suppose, as she said.

But I'll take it. And while I thought I wouldn't be able to sleep, I slide into a deep dreamless slumber with my wee free use wifey at my side.

It's an idyllic two days at Lochside, and I don't care that I can't touch Blythe, because we're too busy having fun. She's delighted with the castle, and marvels over the circular turret rooms with heavy red velvet curtains and the views of the loch through little rhombus glass sections. She makes me show her every room, but there's no question about where she sleeps on Saturday night. It's in my bed, in the warmth of my embrace, her hair tickling my chin.

I thought it would be impossible to control myself now I've had her, and the desire is there, a bulge in my trousers or thankfully hidden by my kilt. But I manage because being with Blythe is everything I need.

We walk next to the loch and up over the moor, flopping down into the springy bed of purple heather and watching clouds. We bathe in the underground hot pool and swim—her more briefly than me—in the cold loch. We drink local peaty whisky after a hearty dinner, and it's so easy.

Admittedly, not ideal when Blythe is texting Ainsley, who is curious about why she's in Scotland for the weekend.

Thankfully, Ainsley doesn't ask where I am when she calls, assuming I'm working as usual. But I'm not. I'm finding out about my wife. Asking her serious questions, and silly ones. Telling her she's off her heid when she confesses she once stayed up until six in the morning reading a book about dragons.

On Sunday night, back at the Blackstone house in London, we're still talking, lying in bed when Blythe's phone pings with a message and she checks it.

"Just Ainsley saying goodnight." She discards her phone and snuggles closer. "It's almost one. It's Monday."

My heart stops. She's my free use wife again. "Do you need to sleep?"

"Mmhum," she agrees, but her little wiggle is pure sensuous mischief.

I bring my hand to her hip. Cotton pyjamas, not skin. I push the fabric aside. My cock rises as I touch her naked curves, desperate after two days of not having her whenever I want.

"Mine," I whisper. "*Mine.*"

That's as much as I can claim.

She must never know that I broke my own rule before I'd ever written the advert.

I can't let her suspect that I love her.

I've no idea if I'm relieved or happy or disappointed as I slide my hand further into her pyjama bottoms and push them down her thighs. Because although Blythe straddles me eagerly when I press my hand on her arse to show where she should go, and it feels so good to have her wet heat settling on the tip of my cock, it's not half as intimate as lying in the heather yesterday, not touching.

9

BLYTHE

I'm at the sink, washing champagne flutes that I found in the cupboard—dusty—when Mr Blackstone walks in, pushes up my skirt, and grabs my bottom.

He brings his face down to mine and grazes his lips over my cheek as he kneads the soft flesh and breathes me in. "Lean over."

That command isn't even necessary. Only two weeks married, and I respond to him on total instinct. I'm a Pavlov dog, but his gravelly voice is my bell, his slow thrust into me is my meal, and it's my pussy that salivates. I'm already flooded, and I've pushed back into his hand. I'm eager to obey, bending at the waist.

This is my normal now, and it's delicious. Mr Blackstone doesn't return home to rail me at lunchtime every workday, but I'm so happy when he does.

My new life is everything I dreamed of.

True, I haven't heard much from Ainsley. She texts and says she's fine, but nearly always puts me off to tomorrow if I suggest a chat. She's mentioned friends, and I don't think she knows about my marrying her father, so I suppose she's just busy. I certainly see plenty of photos on social media, and she sends me gorgeous extra images of the sights she's seeing and the food she's eating.

I'm not even slightly jealous, because I have her dad's attention, and he's everything I want. Nothing makes me feel more desired than the way he doesn't wait.

I go to put the glass I'm cleaning aside, because I want to focus on the delicious sensations between my legs. Plus, usually as I come I shake. I lose control of myself.

"Don't let me inconvenience you," Mr Blackstone says, voice husky. "Keep on washing the glasses." His belt buckle clinks. "But don't drop them."

Ohhhh. I bring the glass under the spray from the tap once more.

This is a new thrill: the challenge of doing something else while being utterly distracted by being railed mercilessly by my husband.

He's *using* me as his toy. He's using me as *his toy*.

He strokes his hand over my naked bottom, and there's the rhythmic sound as he jerks himself a few times, looking at my bare pussy.

I know my husband now. I've seen him take that magnificent cock in hand often enough that I recognise the sound.

"My good little free use housewife. Always so wet," he mutters, as though it's a puzzle.

I bite my lip instead of pointing out I'm soaked for him because he is hotter than a grill turned up to maximum in the Sahara Desert.

He thrusts into me impatiently, and the sudden intrusion of his very substantial length and girth hurts. Then it's just delicious stretch and my clit humming.

I keep washing the glasses, warm water flowing over my

hands and the sunlight from the window making rainbows over my arms. The focus required to continue with the task wars with the instinct to give in to pure enjoyment of how he's ramming into my pussy.

He's fucking me fast and hard, and I'm moaning as he hits some magical place, when a sound like a fire alarm emits from his phone.

He swears colourfully, and still inside me, still thrusting, pulls the phone from his pocket and answers.

"Yes."

I squeal and lose control of the glass I'm holding, and it shatters against the one ceramic side of the sink. My pulse leaps with fear—Mr Blackstone said not to break the glass and probably they're really expensive. What if he stops and tells me off? The idea of his disapproval is jagged in my blood.

"Yes," he repeats into the phone.

He reaches around me and removes the remnant of the broken glass from my hand, before he thrusts again.

I'm paralysed, but he keeps fucking me.

"What?"

Thrust.

I try to stay quiet, I really do.

Thrust.

A whine escapes my closed lips. Released from their duties, my hands ball into fists on the edge of the countertop. I don't know how he's still so hard, or why this is such a turn-on. My climax is just out of reach, nearly there.

Thrust.

So close. Only one more would...

"I'll be there immediately."

A click from his phone, and I expect another thrust. I wait for him to ram ferociously into me, taking his cruel pleasure, leaving promptly afterwards, his seed dripping down my thigh.

He pulls out.

"What...?" I turn to see him tucking his still rock-solid, and as ever massive, cock into his trousers. It's like trying to smuggle a six-foot python. Even as he does up his belt, it's obvious.

I tell myself I can't be upset that work is his priority. I am not upset. I'm not. He's already given up working for two weekends in a row to take me to Lochside.

It's just that I live for these moments when he appears out of nowhere and fucks me as though he was thinking of me—and me alone—all morning.

The aborted orgasm has all sorts of emotions souring my throat. Irrational tears fill my ears. I've failed. I broke the glass. He hasn't come. I haven't provided the relief he needs —that's *my job* to give him—whenever he uses me.

Yeah, I'm a bit frustrated for myself too, of course, but does that alarm mean Duncan is in danger?

Mr Blackstone. Gah. My husband. I don't even know what to call him or how to ask if he'll return home to me or why last week there was blood on his shirt cuff.

This has put me in my place. I'm not a part of his business, or his real life. My stomach sinks. I'm just a convenient free use wife.

I straighten, push my skirt down, and turn. I don't say anything, but I don't meet his eyes either.

Strong fingers pinch my chin and force me to look up into his face. There's a beat of silence. His gaze is serious, cold even.

"Buy two replacement glasses for the broken one."

"But—"

"And a whole new set. Whatever style you like."

"Okay," I reply meekly. I don't want new glasses. What's broken in this relationship is my heart. Stupid girl went and fell in love, and I'll never be that to him. No love was the agreement.

He nods abruptly. Apart from the bulge, you'd never know that thirty seconds ago he was fucking me over the sink.

What did that siren from his phone mean? He's halfway out the door when a single needy word falls from my lips.

"Duncan!"

He pins me with a questioning look over his shoulder, one big hand on the door frame.

It's the first time I've called him by that name, and it shimmers between us. His russet hair has flopped over his forehead, and the dark red and streaks of silver make him appear both hopelessly mortal as well as god-like and powerful. How both are possible, I don't know, but my husband is hot in ways I can't explain.

"Is everything okay?"

His brows pinch together in confusion, as if to say, what do you care? "Fine for me."

I breathe out a shaky sigh of relief.

"London Mafia Syndicate business. The kingpin of Angel is having some trouble with Italian mobsters I've got contacts with."

"Oh." That still sounds dangerous.

"Finish yourself off, Blythe. I'll be checking."

Then he is gone, striding away before I can ask for clarification about what I'm supposed to finish. Cleaning the glasses?

He didn't really mean my orgasm, did he?

And my heart throbs uncomfortably. The Italian mafia. He's not in danger, is he? What if I never see him again?

I've never told him I love him.

I guess it's a good thing I said nothing, because hours later when I'm in bed, he returns home. I'm not asleep, and I don't pretend to be. And I tell him with my enthusiasm for taking his cock as hard and fast, then after that session, sweet as slow, that I love him.

But obviously, he doesn't understand. Because I'm just his convenient free use housewife, and I promised not to expect love.

It was in the advert. *A fake marriage*.

So I don't say the words that repeat in my head: *I love you*.

10

DUNCAN

She's watching television when I get home after a particularly long evening of figuring out some unanticipated and bloody problems. The living room is lit by side lamps, little pools of yellow light that highlight my wife's brown hair. It's casually pulled back in a ponytail as she watches—I'm not sure what it is—a romcom, maybe?

The pale pink strap of her satin nightdress is slipping off her shoulder, and she's curled so cutely on the sofa. For a while I stand in the doorway looking at her. My perfect little forbidden free use wife.

Concern scratches at me, again, about what'll happen when my daughter finds out. Could Ainsley be able to accept her new step-mother? Will Blythe ask for a divorce to try to save her friendship?

I don't think I could grant it. A year seemed like a long time when Ainsley was planning her round-the-world trip, but now it doesn't. A year with Blythe will be over in a blink, and potentially—I hope—she'll have a newborn. We'll have a baby.

That thought calms my nerves slightly. I can't imagine

Blythe not allowing me to see my child, and that means whatever happens, I'll see Blythe.

My wife is special and I cannae resist her.

So I give up my skulking, and walk with deliberate slowness to the sofa. A lie. As though I'm not longing to be by her side.

"Oh, hiya!" Blythe looks up and makes space for me.

I accept the invitation wordlessly, settling into the middle of the couch then pulling her onto my lap.

"How was your day?" She smiles at me expectantly.

"Shh." I touch her chin and smooth my thumb over her lips, turning her face away from mine. It's always easier when her big blue eyes aren't drowning me. "Keep watching your movie."

She obeys, and I shift her small form on my lap, so her legs are apart.

My favourite part of the day is returning home to Blythe, and fantasising that she has been craving me all day as much as I have her. That and shoving her skirt up, and touching her pussy.

"Mine," I whisper into her ear as I cup her pink little slit. And yes... She's slick. My good girl watches the movie, and I look over her shoulder at her tits and dig my fingers deep into her soft velveteen passage. All mine. No one else has ever touched her here. Mine is the only cock to have claimed her.

And she's my toy to give orgasms to.

I do. Over and over, I make her fall apart. I don't let up. I growl with satisfaction when she comes for the first time. She tries to rub herself on my cock, and while I intend to only touch her and not take for myself, I'm weak. So I pull off her scant nightdress, and free my erection, bringing her down onto my cock. I move her on me, lifting her to slam her onto my length and ramming up from beneath.

She's so sexy. It's the little mewling noises that most do it for me.

I hold her waist, reach around, and as I keep fucking into her, the tip of my cock hitting her cervix and my hard-on gripped in her tight wet sheath, I stroke her again. The magic as I feel her come on my cock is just as strong this time as it is every time with us. It's special, the chemistry between us.

When she's collapsed back, her neck exposed, I graze my teeth along her jugular, and I don't stop.

During the next orgasm, she sobs.

The shaking fills me with savage glee, but I really love the uncontrolled cries as she comes for the third time. I just ease off the pressure on her clit and start again, building her up patiently but insistently, kissing her neck and pinching her nipples until she babbles incoherently.

The fourth orgasm tears her apart. Melts her into a puddle on my lap.

My wife is a mess when the end credits of the movie scroll up the screen. She's limp and utterly satisfied, and I finally let myself go. I punch up into her, relishing the cream from her multiple orgasms that has dripped all the way down to my balls.

Slamming her down hard onto my cock, once, twice, three times and allow myself to groan as I fill her up and breed her.

Then I carry my liquid wife upstairs and make her pee before she collapses. I hold her as I wash her in the shower, carefully rinsing her now puffy tender pink folds.

I clean her tenderly, and when I've dried her with a soft fluffy towel, and laid her on the bed and turned off the light,

I intend to let her sleep. But something about the darkness is seductive. When I run my hand down her side, her breath hitches, and she shifts closer. We're both totally naked, since we learned early on that clothes in bed would end up scrunched somewhere and not on our bodies. Except at weekends, when they serve as a useful reminder to me. So I allow myself the indulgence of rolling her under me and making love to her all over again. Face-to-face in the dark.

I mouth the words I want to tell her and don't bother to keep my expression guarded as I do in the light. I try not to take her from the front too much now, because every day I'm closer to giving myself away. Or worse still, seeing something that reveals how she hates what I'm doing.

When we've both climaxed again, and I've cleaned her with a warm cloth this time, I hold her as she falls asleep.

I tell myself that if my daughter issued an ultimatum that it's her or my wife, that I'd let Blythe go graciously. After all, it's only supposed to be a convenient marriage for both of us.

But it's a lie.

I fucking love Blythe so much. I love Ainsley too, but she has her own life to lead. But me? I couldn't live without Blythe. I definitely couldn't rest.

I gather her closer to me, my sleepy warm soft girl. Could I cope if she hated me for ruining her friendship?

She'd be so busy having my babies and taking my cock surely, she wouldn't have any time for loathing. If she was coming constantly, how could she be angry?

That's absolutely false, and I know it. But I draw comfort from the idea anyway. And I resolve to keep her even hornier and make her come more often.

My little free use housewife.

I want her love.

11

BLYTHE

Our first argument as a married couple is caused by clothes. Not even knickers, or not directly. That was cold, at first, not wearing knickers, but my bottom is used to being cold now.

Nope, it was because Duncan wanted me to buy more dresses to wear to the events and evening dinners, he seems to enjoy taking me to. We pretend to be a real couple, of course, me clinging lovingly to his arm and him smiling down at me. Then when we get home afterwards, he's always ravenous. We rarely make it upstairs for round one, and then he licks me out in bed until I scream. Sometimes he wakes me in the middle of the night to breed me again.

Those are the best evenings.

But a little panicky crisis often precedes them on my part. Because he'll arrive home to pick me up, and I'll be ready, and we'll be fine to be on time... And then Duncan will want to fuck me before we go out. Vigorously.

And several times, that enthusiastic coupling has been too much for my dress. It's been ripped, and then we're even more late because I can't figure out what to wear to replace what I carefully chose for the event.

I have pointed out that the most efficient way to solve this is that he gets home before I've got dressed, or that he holds his lust in check until after the evening's entertainment.

Suffice to say, Duncan wasn't impressed by either of those ideas. His solution was just more dresses.

He ordered me to go shopping with an exclusive London personal stylist. Multiples of the same dress if that's what's needed to facilitate what he wants: namely, me.

Which is totally excessive and wasteful, and I told him so.

And he said that if I hadn't spent a hundred thousand on clothes by that time tomorrow and put it on his credit card, there would be *consequences*.

Yes. Well.

Obviously, I spent almost nothing.

I had to know what the consequences were, right? And I was on the moral high ground. Buying dresses so Duncan can rip them when we have sex is ridiculous.

Edging and denial were the punishment. That and spanking. One evening of pink cheeks, and being denied Duncan's cock, and I sobbed I would be his good girl and buy all the clothes he wanted me to.

And that was true. I have spent all of today buying clothes.

Because I really, really need to come. Duncan had strict instructions this morning before he left that I'm not to get myself off. If I don't have him inside me tonight, I'm going to go green, hulk up and explode into goo.

But that doesn't mean I'm his meek little housewife. Ohhh nooo. If I have to buy expensive clothes when I don't think I should? Duncan has to suffer the *consequences* of his actions too.

I've been texting him all day. Every single item I've bought, he has received an image of me wearing it behind the changing room curtain. He edged me so hard I cried, so it's only fair he should feel some of my frustration.

I have bought a lot of knickers. Cute Brazilian cut ones, lacy thongs, and also bras, scandalously short dresses, stockings, skimpy tops, and crotchless knickers. And yes, I made sure to photograph those in their *full* glory.

Pinging over the first picture, I grinned when I saw the tick turn blue and knew he'd seen it. He looked at every single image, but didn't respond.

I admit, I'm excited to see what he's going to do when he gets home later.

I'm unpacking my haul into my wardrobes in our large and airy bedroom, expecting I have plenty of time until Duncan returns, when a door slams downstairs and quick steps thud on the stairs.

My pulse leaps as Duncan strides into the bedroom.

His face is thunder.

"Blythe." A single, furious word. He's across the room and has me pinned to the wall in a second. "You wee fucking, tease."

Then his mouth is on mine, an angry kiss that's possessive. His fingers pinch at me, bruisingly hard and I whimper and try to wriggle away. He ignores me, holding me tighter.

"You think that was funny, huh?" he says against my lips as he wraps his hand around my throat.

My heart pounds as he squeezes, and I gasp for breath. The sensitive part of my windpipe compresses, and I scrabble ineffectually at him.

"Yes."

"Oh, Blythe," he sighs regretfully as he releases my neck, and grabs my dress.

I cry out as he rips it down, the stitching digging into my skin then giving up with a harsh rending, leaving my breasts bared. Ducking to my chest, he bites the sensitive bud of one nipple and pain and pleasure flare out and down my spine.

That distracts me and the next thing I know he's got his trousers open and he's shoving the remnants of my dress from my shoulders so I'm naked, and hitching my thigh to his waist.

"Look what you did to me," he fumes as he fits the crown of his achingly-hard cock to where I'm soft and wet and needy. "I've been trying to work, wifey. And you've been—" he breaks off and thrusts brutally into me, filling me in one stroke.

Our groans fill the air together, mine high and with the pinch of hurt that always happens as he pushes that massive length into me, and his a low rumble of satisfaction.

"Fuck, Blythe." He thrusts again and again, interspersing deep long strokes with short hard flexes of his hips. "The things those photos did to me."

I find his shoulders and cling to him, digging in my nails as the pleasure spirals in me.

"Oh no you don't," he growls as my inner muscles clench, close, so close to orgasm.

He pulls out and roughly jerks me around, pushing my breasts against the wall and pulling my hips back before slamming in again. My nipples are pert from rubbing against his shirt, and the cool wallpaper is just enough stimulation as he takes me hard and fast.

"I guess it's not so funny, now." He's gripping my hip with one hand to keep me in place, and grasps my hair with the other as he grinds out dirty words about how he's wanted to be in my hot wet cunt all day. About how he wanted to use me and feel me come all over his dick.

It's not funny, no. But it's so sexy I can't breathe. I can't say anything. My head is cotton wool, and I can't even remember what I did to deserve being railed so well.

Dominant. Masculine. This man is my husband and so insanely sexy.

"Say you needed this, Blythe," he demands. "You goaded me, you teased me. You got the cock you wanted, didn't you?" He punctuates this statement with short intense thrusts and reaches around to my clit, finding it with total assurance and stroking me.

It only takes that touch. I explode.

"I can feel you coming on my cock, wife." He sounds strained. "Did you fantasise that I'd do this to you?"

"Yes, yes," I babble. "Please." The way he's so hard inside me is unimaginably perfect. Better every time. "I want it. I asked for it, please."

"Good girl," he breathes, and changes to long, smooth thrusts.

I glow from his praise, arching into him.

"Oh you like that do you?" His grip on my hair tightens. Bringing his lips to my ear, he growls, low and rough. "You're being such a good girl for your unhinged, possessive husband. Taking his cock whenever he needs your tight pussy."

A full body shiver of pleasure washes down me from his words.

"I'm going to fuck a baby into your flat belly, my good little housewife. Then another, and another. I'm going to breed you constantly."

I can't help it. I whimper.

The feel of his cock stroking me is phenomenal. I crave it.

"When the weather warms up, I'm going to use you in the garden, in the dirt, pushing you into the ground as I come inside you, and you can't say no."

I don't want to say no. That's the thing. He pretends he doesn't check that I'm wet enough and scan my face for uncertainty every single time he does this, and I pretend that the only reason I let him fuck me is because of this marriage of convenience.

I think he's lying as much as I am. While Mr Blackstone said he didn't want love to be a part of this, he's so loving. He called it free use, but more often than not he makes me come multiple times, before he fills me up.

"One night without being in your pussy *when I could have*, and I'm wild." He speeds up, pounding into me, his movements gone erratic and uncontrolled.

I sneak a look over my shoulder and he looks crazed. His face is screwed up in almost pain. It's a stark contrast to his usual expression of intense focus.

"Don't make me do that again, Blythe. Please." He's hoarse. "I need you."

"I won't." The promise is out of my mouth before I can stop it. Does this mean he finds my days off as difficult as I do?

"Just be my good girl." He makes the request through gritted teeth as he pounds into me harder and harder.

"I will, I will." I can't bear to see him so pained, even as I'm ecstatic that he cares so much and is losing control for me. I'm proud to have made him admit what we both know —*he needs me*.

That's enough.

"Good girl." He chokes out the praise for me as he rams

home with bruising force once, twice, then a third time and he's in me deeper than ever and I feel his dick pulse and the seed I so desperately want hit my cervix as he climaxes in waves.

It triggers another orgasm in me, and he groans as I clench around his length. I see stars. I feel special and powerful to have made this older, experienced, and gorgeous mafia boss lose his cool and unload so much come into me that it's seeping down my inner thigh even as we're both recovering from our orgasms.

"You earned that," he murmurs.

He slides out of me, and the emptiness is immediate. I miss him. Grasping my shoulders, Duncan turns me around, so I face him, my back on the warm patch of the wall my breasts were pressed to. One hand steadying me from the hip, it takes a second to realise that his trousers are still on his thighs. This man wanted me so much—even after weeks of free use to take the edge off—that he didn't bother taking his clothes off.

Then there's something cool and solid at my pussy entrance. I glance down to find my husband with his hand between my legs, smirking at me, a black silicone toy pushing upwards.

He pushes it into place, effectively plugging me.

"I want my seed in you all the time," he states, as though this is totally logical. "I decided you needed a stopper."

Oh my god. It's small compared to Duncan, but my greedy pussy sucks onto the silicone and with the come in me it's a contrast of hot and cool, wet and firm that's decadent. And it's from Duncan. That makes it perfect. I love it.

"Yes, husband," I whisper.

His grin widens. "And there's an extra bonus." Pulling up his trousers and underwear in one, he slowly buckles himself up. Then, reaching into his pocket, he pulls out a remote control.

Oh. Shoot.

It's then that I notice part of the plug is right over my now-sensitised clit.

"I can do this any time, from any distance," he says conversationally as he punches a button with his thumb and the toy buzzes to life.

I cry out, doubling over as the vibrations wrack me, so good it's almost painful.

"That's it," he croons, guiding me to the bed and laying me down as he ramps up the intensity. "It upset you that you couldn't come all day? Well. I'll make up for it. I'll make you come whenever you like."

"Uugghhh."

"Or whenever *I* like." His smile is downright sinful. "And if you send me horny nudes, wifey..." He flicks his thumb on the remote and the vibrations increase again, too much on my clit, forcing me nearly to... "I might decide to get my own back."

I'm coming again, shaking and shouting as Duncan stands over me, drinking in my peak with a satisfied expression.

"That's it." He caresses my knee tenderly as I break apart with this orgasm. It's not as good as the ones with him inside me—sharper and more intense but without the depth and sweetness—but it tingles right to my toes all the same. And Duncan watching on, doing this to me with utter calm after he was shattered only minutes ago, is magic. He eases down the vibrations in sync with my climax, and I'm left lying on the bed, still totally naked as he slips the remote back into his pocket. A threat and a promise.

Then he leans over and climbs on top of me, holding

himself aloof. He cups my jaw and strokes my cheek, looking into my eyes, the blue in his irises as endless as the sky.

"I love..." He pauses and for a moment I'm sure—so sure—that he is going to say, "you". But he tilts his head and gives me a rueful smile. "That you bought underwear."

Disappointment crashes through me, a tropical disease that brings me back to reality.

"Those white lace ones are quite beautiful. But, Mrs Blackstone, I haven't changed my mind. You still can't wear knickers."

12

DUNCAN

She makes dinner for me. We have a chef, but this weekend she told me she was arranging the food for our trip to the Lochside house in Scotland. She has insisted on cooking, and wearing a dress like a mid-century housewife. Blythe has the naughtiest smile tonight.

On a normal weekday evening, I rail my wife as soon as I walk in the door, but our time at Lochside is totally different. I almost look forward to her weekends off where we talk and spend time together without my lust making the whole thing filthy. It's a break from some of the guilt.

Some.

This is our fourth weekend away, and we eat and drink at the solid oak table, flirting over the candles and the delicately-prepared food that I compliment extravagantly. It's not as good as what the chef cooks, but I love that Blythe has done this. She preens at my compliments, and I can tell she's pleased that I'm happy.

My gaze lingers on her waist when she gets up to clear our plates from the main course. I don't help as I would usually, because she seems to have this idea about being my housewife that she wants to take care of me.

And far be it from me to remove any joy of my wife's.

"Here's dessert." She gives me a proud smile as she places a perfect little creation of meringue and fruit and cake and flowers before me.

"That looks amazing. Nowhere near as good as you, but delicious all the same," I tell her with a wink. Then I frown as I notice there's only one portion. "What are you having for dessert? Didn't you make yourself one?"

"Nope. I'm having a different dessert."

"What is this bullshit!" I explode. "Is this about your weight? I've told you before..."

She's laughing at me as lowers herself down before me and, ducking beneath the table, slides her little hands up my thighs.

"Blythe."

Reaching for my belt, she undoes it with nibble fingers, and I can't breathe.

"What are you doing?"

"Getting *my dessert*." She's all sultry heat that goes right to the tip of my cock, where it's straining in anticipation.

I grip the arms of my chair as she nudges herself between my knees.

"It's your weekend off," I said stupidly. We're in Scotland, and I've grown accustomed to compartmentalising this time away from our passion during the week.

"I know."

"Free use only goes one way," I remind her. "I initiate sex. You don't have to."

"What if I want to?"

There's no oxygen in the room. She *wants* to?

Her face is in shadow, so I can't see her expression, but

her hands push aside the fabric, and my erection bobs up, enthusiastic for this turn of events. She wraps a hand around the base, and I bite back a groan.

Pre-come beads at the tip.

Since we agreed this deal was about her getting pregnant, I haven't asked for oral sex. I've given it to her, telling myself it was to make her ready to receive my cock, even as her honey coated my chin.

"You want to give me a blowjob?"

She leans forwards and my cock twitches as her warm breath shivers across the helmet.

"Do I need to tell you about the birds and the bees? That won't get you pregnant."

"I don't care." Then her lips touch, kissing the droplet of moisture at the tip, and I'm lost. My head falls back, and I let my hips flex upwards as she licks me, curious as a kitten.

I watch, amazed and so hard it hurts as she tastes me, then twitches her lips thoughtfully.

"Salty."

I bark out a hoarse laugh.

She looks up, eyes wide. "Aren't you going to eat your desert?"

"No."

She scowls, looking like a grumpy mouse and I grin back.

"I'm the first man you'll ever have between your lips, isn't that right?"

She nods.

"Then I'm going to watch every second of my wife swallowing my cock." I didn't think I'd have this sort of treat, so I'll relish it. I know what her pussy feels like—heaven—and I bet her warm, wet throat is just as good.

Pressing her lips to the length, she eases back and flicks

her gaze between my face and my cock. "I don't exactly know…"

"Put your mouth over the top. Suck me."

Blythe complies eagerly, and it's a second before, "Cover your teeth," is a required instruction.

Then the first couple of inches of my cock are in her mouth and her hands caress the rest of my length and feels *fucking amazing*.

"My clever little wifey," I say, and she hums with contentment. I groan in response and my god, nothing could ever be as beautiful as Blythe giving me this gift.

"Do you want my cock in every orifice? You've taken it in your pussy, plenty, haven't you?"

"Mmm." She agrees with another sound from low in her belly as she bobs and takes me deeper.

"Want my come down your throat too, my good little whore of a wife?"

She gets into a rhythm, and pleasure pools at the bottom of my spine.

"That feels amazing, Blythe. You're doing such a good job."

She looks up at me and I'm crazed. I love her so much.

"I want to paint you with my seed once you're pregnant, bonnie girl. When you're swollen with my baby, I'll claim you again by coming over your luscious tits, and your pretty pink folds."

I don't think I'm going to last long. My wife isn't experienced or expert, but I can see down her dress and see her eyes, the whites showing large, and her pupils dilated as she takes me more and more into her throat. And it's not the blow job, exactly. It's the fact it's Blythe doing this for me. Unprompted.

She's working at her task of getting me off—into her

mouth, nothing in it for her—with single-minded dedication.

"Go on. Do it." I comb my fingers into the hair at the back of her head and slowly press into her scalp, showing her the speed and depth I need. "Make me come. Get it all for yourself to swallow down, greedy girl."

She whimpers in agreement as I move her faster on my cock.

"I'm going to put that pretty dessert onto your belly and force you to keep it still as I eat out your delicious pussy on this table once you're finished, Blythe. I'm going to fuck you with my tongue until you come all over my face."

She's shaking with exertion.

"Are you wet for me, little slut?" My voice is raw as my control slips. I thrust upwards into her mouth, hitting the back of her throat hard. Then I'm unravelled.

"Blythe." Her name is all I can say as orgasm sweeps over my body. My hands are fists in her hair, and it must hurt, but she doesn't object as I pour into her.

No, my free use off-duty housewife swallows down every drop. And when I'm done, a cracked, destroyed, mess of a man, she sits back on her heels and smiles up at me.

13

BLYTHE

We're late to the London Mafia Syndicate meeting because we had sex. Duncan took one look at me in this evening gown, pushed me up against the wall, and had me right there in the hallway. Thankfully, he didn't rip anything this time, and let me get away with only two orgasms.

And while now, I'm as flushed pink as the exceptionally-expensive bright-flamingo silk of my dress, I don't complain as everyone turns when we walk into the private function room in an exclusive hotel in Westminster.

The truth is, when Duncan unbuckles his trousers as soon as he sees me, I'm delighted. When he comes inside me, I'm so content.

He appreciates me. I'm sure of that now.

Okay, he doesn't love me, but...

Yes, that is an issue. Especially because after a month of breeding me, Duncan seems to have achieved exactly what he wanted: I'm pregnant.

My period was due yesterday, and it was a bit optimistic, I guess, but when I didn't see anything, I went straight to the shop and bought a test.

Four. I bought four.

Multiple sticks were peed on, and all said the same thing. I don't know if I'm elated, or terrified, but mostly I'm both.

"It's okay," Duncan says, rubbing my shoulder as I nudge closer to him. He heads towards a group of men standing around, some holding pints of beer or glasses of amber scotch, others just chatting and laughing, hands in pockets, or discussing something serious, pouring over a tablet.

"Ah! This is our new recruit!" A girl with long blonde hair that falls in loose curls halfway down her arms sashays up to us before we can reach the group of men.

I blink. They know about me?

"Welcome to the London Mafia Smut Club." She takes my arm. "You don't mind if we steal your wife, do you?" It's a rhetorical question, clearly, because she's towing me away from Duncan.

I glance over my shoulder, but he's watching with laughter in his eyes, and mouths, "Be good."

"Now." My girl-captor pulls me down onto a squishy sofa on the other side of the room. "Not everyone is here for our book club this week. Some bugs are going around the kids." There are a dozen women lolling on sofas, some who are familiar from the many events with Duncan. They are mainly in formal evening dresses like me, but most have eReaders, and one is absorbed in a paperback with a cartoon of a hockey player on the cover. They look up as I sit.

"Everyone, this is Blythe Blackstone. Blythe, this is—" She rattles off names and London mafia territories that I don't catch because I'm blown away at being described as Blythe *Blackstone*. I know I've been married for a month.

I'm really Duncan's wife, in the eyes of the world, at least. They all smile as though they're happy to meet me.

"So, do you read smut, or do we have to persuade you?" Anwyn, the blonde who fetched me, asks.

"I like to read spicy books," I admit.

"Excellent, so we can go straight to gossip." Anwyn smiles and takes a sip of her drink and pins me with a look and leaving an inviting silence.

"It's so sweet to have another age-gap love match," Felicity, a girl with black hair and soft grey eyes, says, ignoring Anwyn.

"It's not." My heart aches to admit it, but they seem nice. "It's a sham. He wanted a wife..." I can't bring myself to say "to fuck", though that's the truth of it. "And I wanted a husband and family. It's just a marriage of convenience."

Wow, I'm pathetic. Better than saying I'm in love with my husband and he was only looking for a woman of my height and colouring to slake his considerable needs on. Multiple times a day. With orgasms for me as well, seemingly as a matter of honour. He's an excellent husband by every standard—rich and generous, kind and attentive in bed, considerate out of bed. It's not his fault that I pine for his love.

"Not a love match." Felicity snorts. "I've heard this story before from Lina."

"Blackstone is looking at you as though he'd devour you whole, but he's not in love." Lina, the other black-haired girl, hers in a high ponytail, laughs. "Sure."

"No, really, it's just—" I protest.

"Trust me, when a man looks at you like that, what's going on for him is far from *convenient*," Anwyn cut me off. "I remember that expression on Benedict's face when he was still trying to keep to some arbitrary standard of honour and stay away from me because I used to date his son."

Ohhh... I look at Anwyn anew. "And now you're married, and it's for real?"

She smiles happily. "And got babies to prove how real."

That doesn't comfort me. Because I've got the beginnings of a baby, and that's the reverse of proving it's genuine. I wish...

I glance over at where the men are sitting around in various states of tension and ease. I find the tall figure of my husband immediately. His auburn hair makes him stand out, as does the dark-green shirt he's wearing that makes him appear like an excellent tree I'd love to climb.

"Angel, if you can't keep your temper—" The Brent leader raises his voice, sounding very much as though he's the one losing his temper.

"You gavno Italians!" says a Russian-accented voice. "She could have died!"

"Brent can't take responsibility for all the Italian mafias any more than I can for the Scottish." Duncan has clearly taken on the role of peacekeeper in this situation, which is pretty amazing given the number of times I've seen him return home covered in blood.

"I'm trying to help," Brent snarls back.

Duncan sighs and stands. "Maybe you could—"

The Russian pulls out a gun and three things happen at once: a shot is fired, my heart attempts to escape from my chest via my mouth but gets caught at the neck, I dive across the room in a futile attempt to do something heroic and foolish, Duncan rolls his eyes, and the kingpin of Westminster says, "For fuck's sake, do you Bratva have no respect for decorum?"

I'm propelled forward by pure instinct. I have to save Duncan.

How would I save him? I have no idea, and that's impressed on me when every one of the tall, suited, mafia bosses turn to look at me.

I come to a halt in front of Duncan, who looks down at me in alarm and surprise. "What's the matter?"

I'm shaking with fear, that's what. I'm terrified and unable to speak.

There was a gun fired and Duncan was mere feet from danger. I see the Westminster kingpin snap something and the Russian puts away his weapon with a grumble.

It was... No, it wasn't nothing. Duncan could have been killed and all I'd have is his baby and not enough memories.

I can't cope.

"Blythe?" Duncan demands.

I turn. The first step is just fast, my legs tangling in my dress. Then within a second I'm running, and there are the signs for the ladies' toilets, and I barge in and my god it must be the pregnancy hormones because I've never felt so panicked and scared and ready to take on a stupid gun that would kill me easily to protect my husband who doesn't need my help.

I'm an idiot and tears prickle behind my eyes as I throw myself into a toilet cubicle and lean my forehead against the smooth papered wall, the floral pattern swimming before my eyes.

A door slams.

"Blythe." Duncan's voice is urgent and low and something I've never heard before from him. He beats on the door to my cubicle. "Blythe!"

Scared. He sounds as terrified as I was when I thought he was in danger. When I believed for one horrible, leaden moment that my husband might die and my lizard brain wanted to protect him at all costs.

My convenient husband, who hasn't told his daughter about me. I'm a fraud, who didn't understand the most important line in his advert.

No love.

Whatever Felicity saw, she's wrong.

"Blythe!" Duncan slams his palm on the wood. "Let me in *right now* or I'll break the door down."

14

DUNCAN

She opens the stall and I know I shouldn't, but I yank her out of there and give in to my need to shout.

"What were you doing?!" My terror that something was really wrong, that she was hurt, that she was running away from *me*, is excessive. I don't even know what I thought, except that I was convinced I'd lost her, and my fingers dig into her arms. That fucking pink dress. It's gorgeous and I love it and I'm going to rip it off her, to see her bare skin just to calm myself down with a ruthless possession of her. She can wear nothing but my dinner jacket home, I don't care.

"I was upset!" she yells back, surprising me.

"What about?" I'm shocked into a normal tone.

"I was scared that you might die!" She fights me off, her mouth creased with what seems to be genuine distress. Her cheeks are pink and blotchy, matching her dress in colour if not texture. I'm baffled as she shakes, her shoulders hunched, and she averts her face. Hiding from me.

Then it's all clear.

"It's okay. You'd have half my estate, shared with Ainsley, even if you're not pregnant." I reveal what's in the prenup without thinking, because it's understandable she's distressed. She has no idea the lengths I've gone to ensure she's safe.

That very reasonable comment doesn't hit the right spot.

"You idiot!" she sobs, turning and pummelling my chest with her fists. It doesn't hurt, but what does cause me pain is that she's crying now, tears flowing down her pretty cheeks. "Not because of that. Because I love you!"

Every cell in my body stops. My heart ceases to beat. I don't breathe. The shock incapacitates me until the literal lack of oxygen forces me to suck in air before I pass out.

Even so, my head swims.

"It's okay," she mutters, as though she hasn't turned my universe upside down. "You don't have to say it back. Nothing has to change."

"Everything has changed." I still haven't moved.

"I'm just your *convenient* free use house—"

I growl and grab her chin when she casts her gaze down. "You're not *just* anything."

She doesn't reply.

"You're my world," I confess rawly. "Since you turned up on my doorstep, my heart has been yours. I love you more than you'll ever know."

Her mouth falls open, jaw slack with disbelief, and her chin slowly rises until her blue eyes are on me, wide and incredulous.

"Is this because I'm pregnant?"

Is my wife trying to give me a heart attack today?

"You're really pregnant?" It's been a month of filling her with my seed, but I suppose I didn't trust that she would want this like I do. I told myself it might be nothing to her, or a way of placating her demanding husband.

I have been very demanding.

"I'm definitely pregnant." And her smile confirms it. A slow, radiant smile that lights her face from the inside.

My heart expands so much there's no room in my chest for my lungs. No stomach either. Nothing but love for Blythe and the family we'll create together.

"I love you," I confess again. "I never stop thinking about you. I'm going to take such good care of you and our baby."

I pull her into my arms and lean back against the sink as she snuggles into me. And for the first time since we got married, I just hold her.

"I love you too," she says into my chest—she's ridiculously tiny—right to my heart. It hears. Soaks that good shit up like a plant taking on water.

"I've wanted and loved you from the first time we met," I say roughly. "I fell hard and fast, and I've been desperate to admit how much I love you. I've tried to tell you with orgasms."

She splutters with laughter, but nods. "Me too."

I truly hold her close as I've wanted to for this entire month. I squeeze her too tight, like I'd unzip my skin and tuck her safe inside with me. This woman is my everything.

"I'm not going to stop saying 'I love you' with orgasms, Blythe." Grabbing her arse, I hitch her up my body and she clings onto me, her thighs pressing into my waist. I have a hard-on now, because Blythe is my perfect aphrodisiac, but I don't act on it. Just hold her to me, feeling the heat between us rise. I look into her soft palc blue eyes. They still have tears glistening on her lashes, and I'm both glad and furious. "I don't deserve you."

She's already shaking her head, but I stop her with a kiss.

"You'll always be my free use housewife," I tell her between closed-mouth, bruising kisses that I cover her face with. "If you think I've been obsessed with you until now, you're about to see a whole new level now you love me."

"I loved you from the beginning."

"Details." I wrap my arms around her even tighter. "I didn't know. Now I'm going to spoil you as you deserve. I'll love you so much you'll never be able to leave. There'll be nothing convenient about this marriage anymore, Blythe. You've done it. By telling me you love me and you're pregnant, you've guaranteed that you can never even brush past another man for fear I'll kill them for touching you."

This is fully unhinged, but I don't care, because she's making little whimpering sounds of agreement. It's true, and my wife needs to understand. Our temporary marriage was only a small part of my obsession, and she has let me off leash.

"We're going home, and I'll show you exactly how much I love you. Slowly. Thoroughly. I'm going to take you to our marital home, and if you're lucky, we'll end up in our bed before I fill you with all the seed you want. But don't expect to have most of your orgasms in that bed, wife."

"Yes," she whispers. "Yes, to all of that, husband. I'm yours to do with as you like."

I don't put her down, and we don't return to the meeting. They can figure out their nonsense without me. I need to get my wife—who miraculously loves me—home and tell her in more ways that she's my one and only love.

We get as far as the front foyer where we consummated our marriage, and she wiggles in my arms. Because naturally I carried her over the threshold. This is a new start for us. A more honest but no less erotic stage of our love for each other.

"I'm obsessed with your cunt, wife, and I love you more than you'll ever know," I growl as I set her onto her feet and pull up her dress to palm her plump arse. "I'm going to breed you."

"You already did!" she giggles.

"Little free use housewife." I press kisses to her jawline, nibbling at her like I might eat her up. "You're mine and I'll never let you go."

She hums happily.

I'm hard as a rock. My girl is *pregnant*. I got her pregnant, just as she wanted, and I'll enjoy seeing her swell and ripen and be even more gorgeous as a mother.

My wife loves me. Literally everything is better than I could ever have hoped.

"I'll celebrate by filling you with my come, showing you how I love you." I wrap my hand around her neck and hold her to me possessively. "I'm going to make you orgasm on my cock over and over until you're—"

"Dad!" My daughter's horrified voice cuts in. "Oh my god! Blythe, what are you doing? That is disgusting!"

My blood freezes.

We both turn to find Ainsley staring at us in horror.

Shite.

15

BLYTHE

Disgusting. The word echoes in my head.

"I can explain." I pull away, but Duncan doesn't let go. He releases my skirt, and it falls back over my thighs, but he grabs my hand, locking our fingers together.

"Ainsley, what happened?" Duncan rumbles. "Why are you here?"

"Why am I home?" she explodes. "I came to meet your new girlfriend and instead find you're assaulting my best friend!"

"It's not—" I begin.

"Blythe is my wife," Duncan cuts me off.

"Your what?" Ainsley turns to me, confusion and betrayal in her expression. "You two are married?" Her gaze flicks down to my left hand and her eyes go round as she sees my wedding ring and the huge diamond engagement ring.

"Yes," I say with pathetic inadequacy.

"You got married without me?" Shaking her head in disbelief, her face crumples. "You're my dad and my best friend, and you didn't even tell me."

My heart wrenches. Ainsley adopted me when I had no one, and was struggling at university. I owe her everything.

"You said you were in Scotland, and didn't have a job, and I didn't twig." She laughs mirthlessly. "I'm an idiot. You must have had fun laughing at how stupid I am."

"It wasn't like that," I insist. "We were worried about what you'd say."

Ainsley's expression darkens back to rage as she turns back to her dad. "To think I wanted to meet your girlfriend." And despite her anger, I can hear how upset she is that we've kept this from her. "When did you get married? Actually, don't answer that."

I don't respond, because the fact we got married so quickly is the worst part. We've been keeping this from her for a month. But Duncan murmurs the date of our wedding and Ainsley's mouth falls open in shock as she looks at me.

"You've been sneaking around behind my back all this time." Blood drains from her face. "Were you at it while you stayed with me?"

"It happened after you left." Oh god this is a mess. "Not before, I promise." I'm leaden. I feel awful. I want to sink into the floor. Duncan's hand, warm and strong over mine, is the only thing preventing me.

"You screwed my *dad*... Is this for his money?"

"No." The accusation spurs me into a passionate denial. I can't let that stand. Money is the last thing my marriage is about, but I don't think Ainsley will like that I had a sex deal with her father.

"Did you seduce—?"

"I suggest you stop right there before you say something rude about *my wife*," Duncan interrupts her. His voice reminds me more clearly that he's my older mafia boss husband who has a daughter my age. It's deep and authoritative in a way that tells me I'm safe. I'm protected. He'll always be on my side, and he's the big bad.

"You lied to me!" The hurt is in every word she hurls at us.

Ainsley goes to run away, but Duncan stops her with a short, "Ainsley."

The guilt that has been clawing at my insides since the beginning breaks through and tears prickle behind my eyes.

"I'm going to make us tea, and then we're going to talk this through like adults in the lounge."

He's still a dad, I realise as Ainsley trails us into the kitchen. The contrast of the dark of night outside and the white light from the ceiling spots Duncan flicks on is almost painful to my eyes.

"Sit." He instructs a few tense minutes of tea making later, nodding towards the sofa.

"I'm not a dog, Dad," Ainsley grumbles, but does as he says. Duncan ignores her and takes the place next to her on the three-seater.

I go towards the single chair, but Duncan catches my eye and shakes his head, dipping his gaze towards the place on the other side of Ainsley.

And clearly, I'm still his little housewife, because I do as he commands. Ainsley regards us, half confused, half suspicious.

"Why are you home?" Duncan asks as he pushes a cup of tea towards Ainsley and places a plate of chocolate biscuits on the low table.

"Aren't we talking about how you ended up marrying my best friend?" she snips back at him.

"Aye, but first why are you here?"

"I..." Ainsley's voice breaks and she lunges for her tea. Duncan meets my gaze over her head, and there's nothing but compassion and worry and love there. He cares about his daughter deeply.

"What happened?" I ask gently. "Your texts said you were fine?"

"Your texts said you were fine too," Ainsley points out belligerently through a mouthful of sweet milky tea. "You didn't mention you were married!"

I flush.

"You didn't like mainland Europe?" Duncan asks mildly.

"The food is funny," Ainsley mutters, grabbing up a chocolate-covered biscuit and crunching it noisily. "This is the first proper cup of tea I've had in a month."

"Uhuh." Duncan takes a sip of his tea and waits.

"I just..." Ainsley hesitates, then the floodgate opens. "I didn't enjoy it like I thought I would. I couldn't understand the language, no one could understand my accent. I nearly got arrested over a comment supporting my gay friend back home. The accommodation was ridiculous." She pouts and continues with a laundry list of genuine and imaginary complaints.

"I was lonely," she confesses eventually, putting down her tea and placing her hands in her lap. Duncan takes one, holding it in his big paw. "I missed you, Blythe, and now I find you've been shacking up and not thinking of me at all."

"We thought of you," I assure her, taking her other hand and the three of us are connected.

"But not while actually shacking up," Duncan adds dryly. "Why didn't you tell me?"

"Or me?" I ask. "I'd have been there to listen."

Ainsley shrugs. "You both thought I was going on the adventure of a lifetime. I didn't want to be the pathetic girl who wasn't enjoying the trip I'd bigged up so much."

"I wouldn't have thought that, I promise," I tell her.

Duncan and I meet eyes over Ainsley, and the flare of connection is different to our usual sexual frisson. It's the shared knowledge of two people who both love another person, as well as each other. This is parental love, and I know somehow, deep inside of me, that we'll do this again and again. It won't necessarily be with Ainsley, but with our own children who we support through all the lonely trials of life.

That strengthens me.

"Do you still want to go travelling?" Duncan asks.

Ainsley tilts her head and pauses. "Yes."

"Okay. I'm going to call an old friend who lives in America. You can visit him. He'll take care of you. Make sure you have a good time until you've found your feet with travelling and are ready to go solo."

"Really?" Ainsley blinks. "You're not cross?"

"I'm not cross with you."

He's a great dad. I knew it, of course, but with the tiny life growing inside of me the certainty takes on a new importance. He's going to be loving and tender and fiercely protective of our babies.

"How can I be, when you're going to be very understanding of your new step-mother." Duncan's smile is half wry amusement, half hope, and a bubble of hope lifts me.

"Oh god." Ainsley cringes.

"And your half-siblings," he adds.

"You're really serious about this?" Ainsley turns to me, doubt in expression. "You lied to me."

"I'm sorry about the lying." I squeeze my best friend's hand. "It was stupid. But I love Duncan, and I was scared you'd react badly."

Her eyes widen for a split second at me calling her dad

by his first name. "Well... I guess I know now and..." She shakes her head in confusion. "I don't get it, but if this is what you want..."

"We're very serious about the siblings," Duncan adds, deadpan.

"Oh no. Make it stop." But Ainsley is laughing, and the tension in my chest eases. "I don't need to hear any of the details. If you're happy—"

"We are." And it's easy to talk for both of us, because it's true. I'm utterly secure in my husband's affection now.

Duncan catches my eye above Ainsley's head, and his expression has softened with the emotions he's kept hidden, but have bled out around the edges over the last month. Now he's told me, I can see all the ways he showed his feelings. With orgasms, yes, but in other ways too.

I can't wait to go back to Lochside with all three of us together. And in nine months' time, with our baby too.

"I love you," he mouths.

"Just because I'm not mad with you anymore, doesn't mean you can start smooching in front of me." Ainsley glances between us. "Cut that out, you two."

Duncan grins. "Not a chance."

EPILOGUE
DUNCAN

9 YEARS LATER

I'm in my home office on the phone to my chief financial officer when there's a roar of young voices and three children fall into my office, scrapping like street urchins and yelling, "Death to the dragon".

Or something? I think.

"I'll call you back."

I sigh as I put the phone down and regard my offspring brawling on the floor. These three are our eldest. Skye is eight, Rory seven, Lainey is six. Our youngest is just two, and I have a pang of longing for my sticky little toddler and her precious milky scent.

"Dad, they aren't playing fair!" Skye complains, looking up from the pile of red and auburn-haired children.

"What's the problem?" I ask.

They all start babbling at once.

"I'm the princess," declares Rory.

"No, I'm the princess!" says Lainey. "You're the dragon!"

"I thought we were all dragons this time?" Skye looks very put out.

Mafia disputes have nothing on siblings.

"You all seem to have swords. Are you all knights?" I suggest, nodding to the rulers they're brandishing.

Skye gives me a withering look. "Dragons can have swords, Daddy."

"Dragons have opposable thumbs in this game?" They all blink at me, bemused and affronted by my attempt to impose logic on their fantasy game.

"This." I waggle my thumb. "You need it to pick up things. If you look at the dog, you'll see he can't do that."

Skye tilts her head curiously, and considers. "Our dragons have opposable claws."

"Good. Glad we cleared that up." Now if we could just ascertain why my children feel it's fine to bring their game into my office mid-morning on a Tuesday, we'd be all set. But that's not really a question. The reason is me.

They like turning up at odd times to see *me*.

Weird. But no accounting for taste.

I wanted more kids, I asked Blythe for kids, and I adore every creature Blythe brings to our house. Even that dog she rescued when we agreed six was enough babies. We said five children, but she was so beautiful pregnant, I bred her with one extra.

Thankfully, we have grandchildren too, after Ainsley found her happiness in the US on her trip. I wasn't impressed by her choice at first. In fact, I was downright murderous. But she was very certain, and who am I to stand in the way of love, even if it's taboo…

I guess I'm too indulgent of all my children. I've never

set limits for them. The change from working out of the house mainly to setting up an office at home was right after Skye was born, and so they've barely known times when I'm not available to listen to their problems. They're welcome to interrupt me anytime, because as important as my work is, my children and grandchildren are more essential. Them and my wife. I'm still rather obsessed with Blythe.

A recollection from last night flickers. Blythe, under me. We don't have as much time and space for free use as before the kids arrived, but we find and make opportunities. Stolen moments at night, or when the children are with their nanny. I still pull Blythe into the bathroom for a quickie or follow her into the garage and lock it behind me for time alone.

The kids regroup after their mini-brawl, seemingly agreeing they are all dragons now. Or dragon riders? I'm not entirely sure, or certain if I contributed to this decision. Rory and Lainey run off, flapping their "wings" and I settle back to resume my phone call.

"Oh, Dad, Mum says lunch is ready," Skye says as she looks after her brother and sister.

I jerk my head up. "What?"

"Yeah, we were supposed to bring you a message," she says with a nod, as though I should have known. "Lunch is ready."

I choke a laugh. "But it's only..."

A check of my watch reveals, no it is not mid-morning. It is after twelve.

Smiling, I follow my motley wee dragon crew into the kitchen. The scent of garlic and cream is wafting in the air. Blythe is wearing a frilly apron with a little flower pattern and has just settled our youngest into a highchair. My wife is so gorgeous. After nine years together, she's more beautiful in my eyes than ever. She looks up and sees me, her face brightening into a smile. It's only a few hours since we were together in bed, her coming as I licked her out. But nevertheless, she's pleased to see me. She lights up.

My heart expands and I'm at her side in a moment, sweeping my hand into her hair and drowning—again—in her blue eyes. Or maybe it's soaring through the sky.

"Hello, wife," I murmur before I take her mouth in a kiss. Around us the kids complain that they think their parents are behaving unacceptably.

I don't care. I kiss Blythe in front of them all, frequently, because they're a product of our love, and should know that love is nothing to be ashamed of. Ever. Plus, they should see that affection between a couple is normal.

Blythe presses close to me, and where the kids can't see, I skim my hand over her arse. Familiar lust mixes with satisfaction. No knickers.

My wife never wears knickers.

The kids have given up waiting and grumbling and are tucking into their lunch by the time I break our kiss.

And as Blythe meets my gaze, her lips tilt upwards in a private little smirk between the two of us. Because she knows there will be more of that kiss for us later.

"Mine," I whisper, low enough the kids won't hear. "Mine."

My free use housewife. Forever.

EXTENDED EPILOGUE
BLYTHE

A hand sweeps possessively down my side, then there's heat and a solid body at my naked back.

I'm drugged with sleep, unable to open my eyes or rally my mind.

"Sweet little fucktoy."

My upper leg is lifted, and something hard presses at my revealed entrance.

There's a pinch and I shift, trying to get away in confusion.

"Don't fight it, lass." The hard object retreats, then warm moisture is smeared between my legs.

I'm half asleep. Or dreaming. I can't tell which.

Fingers hold my leg, and a bicep I hadn't realised I was using as a pillow tightens as he presses his hand to my chest.

"Good girl. You can stay asleep while you take it."

Then an unyielding length pushes at my entrance. Between his hand at my chest, holding my thigh, and how sleepy I am, I can't resist. He breaches me.

He groans as he withdraws and thrusts in deeper. "Don't move. You feel so good."

The pinch of pain from his size eases as I accommodate him, stretching for him. I'm still so sleepy I can barely move. My mind is fogged because I was so far down.

But when his hand finds my breast, and grasps it roughly, it's not for my pleasure, it's for *his*. I'm being a warm, willing, soaked hole for him to slake his lust on, and generous tits for him to enjoy.

My husband loves my breasts. Maybe even more since we've had children, because they're bigger and frequently plump with milk. He squeezes the soft flesh, my puckering nipple in his palm as his thumb strokes.

At first, he goes slow, as though he's trying not to wake me fully. He nuzzles my neck, all the time moving inside me. His breath is hot as he sucks the flesh there until I cry out. Then his dark chuckle causes my clit to throb, and she shifts to kissing the back of my head.

His thighs smack onto mine as he moves faster, bottoming out, filling me up.

"My pretty fucktoy. You're so good at this, taking my cock. Such a good girl."

I love these early morning free use moments. I'm barely awake, and I'm providing for my husband perfectly. He's telling me over and over how pleased he is with me, how I'm his good girl, how hot it is that I'm not resisting.

All I have to do is lie here and feel the orgasm rising in me. He fills my senses. Big inside me, as ever, stretching me out deliciously, but also the scent of sex and his aftershave is around me. The taste of his come is still on my lips from last night when I sucked his cock, his hand fisted in my hair. It's dark and shadowy in our bedroom, but the touch of the sheets is lovely against my naked skin.

Even after years of marriage, free use is still freeing. It is a lack of responsibility that's how I imagine soaring through the sky as a bird would be.

I love our family. The six children that I tempted him into giving me, and the pets that he indulges my coming home with. They're a lot of work, and responsibility. And even though the Blackstone mafia has more allies now than enemies, Duncan is often working. I adore our life, even when it's a lot.

But these times, when it's just me and him, he takes all the control. I can't worry about anything, because I'm just here for his free use. Nothing else in the world for me to do but open my legs, or my mouth, and tell him, "Yes".

"I love you so much. I cannae resist you." He shoves into me even harder. "Your pussy, fuck, Blythe. It's heaven. Soft, wet. *Mine*. I own you, you ken?"

"Yes." I love saying that. I love being his, and when he uses me and tells me he loves me?

Top tier. Bestest feeling ever.

"Say it," he demands.

"I'm yours," I pant out. "I'm your good girl."

I feel him nod and the purring growl of satisfaction he releases causes warm shivers down my spine. He edges my knee higher, opening me more to him, and slams in even deeper. I can feel him all the way through me. He's right up, under my ribcage, and into my heart.

"That's it. I bought you like a little broodmare, I've bred you, and now you're a little comeslut for me."

I mewl in agreement as the orgasm builds.

"I love every filthy part of you," he says hoarsely, beginning to lose it as his thrusts become more erratic. "I'm obsessed with you, *wife*."

"You're so hard. So big." I'm incoherent. Partly because it's probably five in the morning, but also because my husband's cock makes me stupid. He fills me with cock and come so fully my brains get squished out of my ears.

"Hold yourself open for me," he snarls, and I scramble to obey, hooking my wrist behind my knee. Why becomes immediately obvious. Duncan's fingers are between my legs, circling my clit.

I break without warning and behind me, Duncan groans as my orgasm starbursts out of me in pulse after pulse.

My husband is shaking as he fills me with wet heat, repeating my name and that he loves me over and over.

I'm so close to him, wrapped tightly in his arms, as I gradually open my eyes. The grey-yellow light of dawn is peeking out from between the curtains. We haven't moved, still joined, and the sticky cream covers my thighs, his fingers, and no doubt his cock as well.

"I'm proud of you," he whispers.

I bask in that, my smile of contentment the only muscle that's doing anything in my whole body. Apart from my mouth, I'm unable to move.

"My husband," I breathe. "I'm always happy to be your toy."

"Blythe." He strokes his hand all the way down my side. "I'm proud of that too, but I meant what a good wife and mother you are. You're my world."

"Mine too," I reply and when he kisses the back of my head this time, I know it means he hasn't got the words to explain how grateful he is that we're together.

INSTALOVE BY EVIE ROSE

Stalker Kingpins

Spoiled by my Stalker

From the moment we lock eyes, I'm his lucky girl... But there's a price to pay

Owned by her Enemy

I didn't expect the ruthless new kingpin—an older man, gorgeous and hard—to extract such a price for a ceasefire: an arranged marriage.

His Public Claim

My first time is sold to my brother's best friend

Pregnant by the Mafia Boss

Kingpin's Baby

I beg the Kingpin for help... And he offers marriage.

Baby Proposal

My boss walked in on me buying "magic juice" online... And now he's demanding to be my baby's daddy!

Grumpy Bosses

Older Hotter Grumpier

My billionaire boss catches me reading when I should be working. And the punishment...?

Tall, Dark, and Grumpy

When my boss comes to fetch me from a bar, I'm expecting him to go nuts that I'm drunk and described my fake boyfriend just like him. But he demands marriage...

London Mafia Bosses

Captured by the Mafia Boss

I might be an innocent runaway, but I'm at my friend's funeral to avenge her murder by the mafia boss: King.

Taken by the Kingpin

Tall, dark, older and dangerous, I shouldn't want him.

Stolen by the Mafia King

I didn't know he has been watching me all this time.

I had a plan to escape. Everything is going perfectly at my wedding rehearsal dinner until *he* turns up.

Caught by the Kingpin

The kingpin growls a warning that I shouldn't try his patience by attempting to escape.

There's no way I'm staying as his little prisoner.

Claimed by the Mobster

I'm in love with my ex-boyfriend's dad: a dangerous and powerful mafia boss twice my age.

Snatched by the Bratva

I have an excruciating crush on this man who comes into the coffee shop. Every day. He's older, gorgeous, perfectly dressed. He has a Russian accent and silver eyes.

Kidnapped by the Mafia Boss

I locked myself in the bathroom when my date pulled out a knife. Then a tall dark rescuer crashed through the door... and kidnapped me.

Held by the Bratva

"Who hurt you?"

Before I know it, my gorgeous neighbour has scooped me up into his arms and taken me to his penthouse. And he won't let me go.

Filthy Scottish Kingpins

Forbidden Appeal

He's older and rich, and my teenage crush re-surfaces as I beg the former kingpin to help me escape a mafia arranged marriage. He stares at me like I'm a temptress he wants to banish, but we're snowed in at his Scottish castle.

Captive Desires

I was sent to kill him, but he's captured me, and I'm at his mercy. He says he'll let me go if I beg him to take his...

Printed in Dunstable, United Kingdom